MARINE
FOR HIRE

A FRONT AND CENTER STORY

TAWNA
FENSKE

Entangled Publishing, LLC
2614 South Timberline Road
Suite 109
Fort Collins, CO 80525
Visit our website at www.entangledpublishing.com.

Lovestruck is an imprint of Entangled Publishing, LLC.

Edited by Heather Howland and Kari Olson
Cover design by Heather Howland

Manufactured in the United States of America

First Edition February 2014

I'm pretty sure it's wrong to dedicate a book to an 8-year-old and a 12-year-old who aren't allowed to read it.
Nevertheless, I dedicate this one to Violet and Cedar for inspiring me to eat my own words after I swore I'd never write a book with kids in it.
Thank you for inspiring me in a million other ways as well, with your infectious laughter, unique perspectives on the world, and personalities that routinely prompt friends and strangers to tell me I won the step-kid lottery. Believe me, I know. And I love and adore the snot out of you guys.
Stop reading here, okay?

Chapter One

The chain saw snarled in Sam's hands. He plunged it into the log, rewarded by the spit of wood chips and a mechanical growl of protest from the machine.

Sam could relate. At least that was his sentiment as the unmarked black car crawled slowly up his father's driveway, drawing closer by the second. Government car, from the look of it. More military officials wanting to discuss what happened in Kabul? Like Sam hadn't already talked about it plenty.

Okay, fine. He hadn't. Still, that didn't mean he was in any mood to do it now.

He killed the chain saw, but kept it in his hands. Might as well look the part of a man who didn't want to be disturbed. He waited, tense but unmoving, as the car eased to a halt in front of him. Its tinted windows reflected the towering pines behind him, along with Sam looking like he'd spent the morning mud wrestling a tree trunk. The passenger took an unnecessarily long time opening the door, and he waited, breathing in the scent of damp leaves and fresh sawdust. The car door swung wide, and an expensive Italian loafer stepped onto the wet gravel driveway, followed by another.

In an instant, the tension drained from his shoulders.

"Holy shit, Mac," Sam said, lowering the chain saw. "What the hell are you doing here?"

Mac got out of the car and took three steps toward him. They clapped each other on the shoulders and conducted a complicated ritual that was equal parts hug and sucker punch to the gut.

Sam drew back first, brushing sawdust off the front of his T-shirt as he surveyed his old pal. Mac wore his usual dark sunglasses, despite the fact that it was an overcast afternoon in the forest outside Portland, as opposed to a beach bar in Jamaica on a summer afternoon. Mac's clothes were black — of course — and the whole suit looked like it cost more than Sam's car.

Sam looked down at his own dusty T-shirt and tried to remember if he'd worn deodorant. Or taken a shower.

"Sam," Mac said, straightening his lapels. "Nice to see you. You're looking good. A little shaggy and rumpled, but it works for you."

Nope, definitely no deodorant. Sam covertly sniffed his own T-shirt and grimaced. Oh well, it was just Mac.

"Military grooming standards weren't exactly required on my last mission," Sam said. "Figured I'd wait on a haircut 'til my leave is up. Not much need for starched uniforms or pressed fatigues out here."

"Good. That's good." Mac nodded with something that looked oddly like approval. "I heard you were up here helping your dad and stepmom get ready for winter."

"Yeah, doing a little caulking, cleaning out the gutters, stockpiling firewood, that sort of thing." He quirked an eyebrow at Mac, not willing to let the statement go unquestioned. "You *heard*?"

Mac waved a dismissive hand, and Sam did a mental eye roll. His friend had unlimited resources when it came to gathering information and pretty much everything else he wanted. It was no secret that whatever Mac did for a living was—well, *secret.*

They'd met playing football in college before the Marines, both ambitious young men driven by overbearing fathers and too much testosterone. Sam had stuck with the program, training as a sniper and making a pretty good career at it.

At least until Sam's whole world had come undone.

Mac, on the other hand, had gotten out of the military and moved on to some sort of top-secret government work that kept him out of the country a lot. Whatever it was he did now, it made him extremely wealthy.

Mac probably never forgets deodorant.

"So," Sam began, brushing his free hand over his dirty jeans. "What's up?"

"You're on leave for another couple weeks?"

He resisted the urge to grit his teeth. "I'm still considering getting out."

"But you haven't dropped your letter. You know damn well it takes a while, and all your shit is still in storage in Hawaii."

"For now."

Mac cleared his throat. "So. What are your plans until then?"

"You're looking at it."

Mac nodded, surveying the property with a calculated expression. "A couple weeks of work. Probably much quicker work if Grant and I pitch in to help. Or we could always hire a crew to come out and—"

"Grant?" Sam asked, confused now. "Isn't your brother stationed in Benghazi right now? And why would he help my parents with yard work?"

Mac turned back to him, and Sam caught his own disheveled image in the reflection of his buddy's glasses. He had a streak of mud on one cheek, and he hadn't shaved all week.

"You like kids, right?" Mac said. "I mean, you have all those nieces and nephews."

Sam frowned. "Sure, kids are great. My sister's having another little girl in April."

He nodded as though making a mental list. "Can you operate an oven?"

"Microwave. Oh, and I baked brownies once. Laced 'em with Ex-Lax as a prank for some SEAL buddies at a party."

"How do you feel about Kauai?"

Sam raised an eyebrow and wondered—not for the first time—if Mac had gone crazy. "Is this some kind of psych exam where you're going to show me ink blots and ask whether I fantasize about badgers wearing men's underwear?"

Mac folded his arms over his chest. He didn't answer the question. "You remember my sister, Sheridan, right? I think you met her once at a party in college."

At the mention of Sheri's name, Sam felt several pints of blood drain from his brain and pulse toward other extremities. He thought about those thick, chocolaty curls and those huge brown eyes, and that perfect, heart-shaped ass and—

"I think I remember her," he said, straining to keep his voice casual. "Blond, right?"

"You know goddamn well she's a brunette, just like I know goddamn well you didn't stop staring at her that whole night at the party. That's not why I'm asking. Her douchebag husband left."

Sam blinked. "What? Didn't they just have a kid?"

"Two kids. Twins. Seven months old, and Lieutenant Limpdick ran off with a stripper he met in Arkansas. We're dealing with the situation."

He refrained from asking who "we" might be or what "dealing with the situation" entailed. Probably best not to know. "Weren't they stationed in Honolulu?"

Mac nodded. "Sheri's still there. Well, on another island now. Kauai. She has a friend there, and she just got a job as an accountant on the Pacific Missile Range Facility."

"Civilian gig?"

"Yeah. Great pay, good bennies. But she's a single mom, and she needs a nanny. A *good* nanny. Someone who can cook and who's great with kids and housekeeping and M40 sniper rifles."

"You got that job description on Craigslist?"

"And maybe black-belt level karate skills," Mac continued, ignoring him. "And the ability to use power tools."

"You can't be serious." Sam shook his head, propped the chain saw against a stump, and rubbed a smear of mud off his forearm.

"Why not? You're supposed to report for your new command in Hawaii in a couple weeks anyway. In the meantime,

Sheri needs someone to watch out for the twins. And her."

He touched one hand to the utility knife on his belt and stared Mac down. Then he remembered it wasn't possible to stare Mac down, especially since the guy never removed his sunglasses.

He tried reasoning instead.

"Aren't there services for this sort of thing? There have to be a thousand people more trained to be nannies."

Mac leaned against a tree, his arms still folded. "No one with your unique qualifications. And not anyone who happens to owe me a favor."

Sam sighed, already knowing how this would end up. "I appreciate you saving my life in Baghdad. I do. But can't I just buy you a beer or a car or something?"

"No."

"I'm not following why you want me looking after your sister and her kids. Why me?"

"She's alone," he snapped. "For the first time in years with two little babies and a new job and a dickhead ex-husband I don't trust. Grant and I are going to be out of the country and our folks are all the way over in Honolulu and God only knows where Schwartz is. None of us will be around to keep an eye on Sheri in Kauai and make sure she's safe."

"Why wouldn't she be?"

Mac ran his hands through his hair, looking rattled for the first time in the whole conversation. "Lieutenant Limpdick is a real piece of work. The divorce didn't go well, and he's still harassing Sheri. His orders have come through, but he's got two more weeks before he has to leave."

"He's still attached to the command in Hawaii?"

"Yes. He'll be back in the islands any day now. While he's there, I don't want him getting anywhere near Sheri and her boys."

"He's dangerous?"

"He's never been physically violent with her, but he's unpredictable. I worry he'll try to win her back and won't take no for answer, or that he'll show up and make life hell for her. He's a manipulative prick and a threat."

"A threat you want controlled."

"Precisely. Look, it's not just the ex, Sam. There are bad drivers in Hawaii. And sharks. Plus Sheri's never been good about locking her doors or windows, and what if—"

"I've got it," Sam said, holding up his hand. "You guys have always been overprotective. This takes the cake, though, even for you."

Mac gave a curt nod. "Our family would feel better if someone we know and trust was looking out for Sheri and the twins." He hesitated, looking uncharacteristically uncertain. "There's one catch."

"Only one?"

Mac ignored him. "Sheri has a problem with controlling military men meddling in her life."

"I can't imagine why."

"She can't know we're sending a bodyguard to watch over her, and she definitely can't know you're a Marine."

Sam shook his head. "Your whole family is military to the core. She'd peg me as a Marine before I got through the front door."

Mac stared him up and down, considering. "Not necessarily. This disheveled look you've got going on right now is working for you. You look like hell."

"Thank you," Sam said. "You're aware that this is insane, right? I don't know how to cook or change diapers or get baby vomit out of cashmere."

"It's Hawaii. No cashmere needed, and baby vomit blends nicely into floral-patterned shirts."

"You're missing the point."

Mac didn't respond, just stared at him through those dark lenses with his hair unruffled in the breeze. "This is your chance to make things right," he said. "After what happened in Kabul, it's how you prove to yourself again that you're a good guy—a guy who knows what it means to serve and protect and follow orders."

Mac's words sliced through him, and Sam's fingers clenched in an unexpected fist. He wasn't sure who he wanted to punch. Himself, mostly.

Sam swallowed. "Sheri needs someone right away?"

"Just for a couple weeks. I'll find her a real nanny when Limpdick's out of the picture. Oh, and there's one other thing."

Sam raised an eyebrow, resisting the urge to remind him that *just one catch* had already morphed into more.

Mac folded his arms over his chest again. "Keep your hands off my sister."

Sam blinked. "What?"

"You heard me. She's vulnerable. With Limpdick out of the picture, she needs time to recover."

He heard a rushing sound in his brain, not unlike the night he met Sheri at that party in college and she'd been wearing that huge, goofy smile and pink lipstick and that crocheted white bikini that hugged her curves and showed the perfect outline of her nipples and Sam had tripped over a piece of driftwood and fallen face-first into all that luscious cleavage and—

"When do I start?"

. . .

Sheridan Patton-Price set two mugs of tea on the table before retreating to the kitchen for the creamer she was pretty sure expired a week ago.

"Um, Sher?" called her best friend, Kelli. "I think you forgot something in the tea."

"What's that?"

"The tea."

"Right." Sheri sighed and pulled two tea bags out of the cupboard. She trudged back to the table and plunked a bag into each mug before dropping heavily into a chair. It was the first time she'd had a moment to sit for—days? Months? How long had the twins been napping?

"You look like you could use this," Kelli said, reaching into her bag and pulling out a flask emblazoned with a Hello Kitty emblem. She splashed a healthy dose in both mugs and replaced the flask in her bag. "Bourbon. The good stuff. Were you up all night again?"

Sheri nodded, pulling off her eyeglasses. She used the temple piece to stir her tea, wondering if *normal moms* had clean teaspoons in the house.

"I think the twins are teething," Sheri said, taking a tentative sip of tea. "How do I know for sure?"

"When they get teeth?"

"Thanks. The only woman in the world who knows less about babies than I do, and I choose to ask her for advice on child rearing."

Kelli beamed. "You're welcome. I consider it my duty to make you feel better about yourself. Want me to show you the cellulite on my ass?"

"I'll take a rain check. Though I do like the idea of looking at an ass I don't have to clean with a baby wipe."

Kelli picked up her mug and knocked back half the contents in one gulp. *Good idea,* Sheri thought, and followed suit. She felt guilty drinking bourbon at noon on a Thursday, but there wasn't much that didn't make her feel guilty these days. For starters, she was pretty sure she was the most ill-prepared mother on the planet. She'd fought valiantly to hide it, beginning the moment the nurse handed her twin boys and Sheri asked numbly, "Are you sure that's a good idea?"

"Am I sure what's a good idea?" Kelli asked.

"What?"

"You're talking to yourself again."

Sheri sighed and tugged at the string on her tea bag. "Sometimes I think there was a day someone handed out all the mothering instincts. All the women got in line, but I couldn't find my keys or my glasses, and by the time I made it there, all they had left was a box of day-old doughnuts and a penchant for complicated algebra."

"I must've been in line behind you then," Kelli said. "That's when they handed out the ability to take care of four-legged creatures instead of two. Makes me a pretty good vet, though."

"At least I can come to you if the twins show signs of ear mites or kennel cough." Sheri took another sip of tea, enjoying the warmth of the bourbon sliding down her throat. "I spent all morning thinking Jeffrey was Jackson and Jackson was Jeffrey. And then I got halfway through putting on their diaper rash cream before I realized it was toothpaste. What kind of mother does that?"

"Well, they *are* twins. And now their little backsides are minty fresh and tingly."

"I joined a Mommy and Me group last week, and the other moms made me feel guilty about using disposable diapers on an island that already has a trash problem. I'm trying to switch to cloth, but do you have any idea how much work it is to wash diapers for *two* babies?"

"I love you, Sher," Kelli said, touching the back of her hand. "And I'll gladly hold your hair back if you need to puke in a barroom toilet on girls' night. But there's no way I'm helping you wash diapers."

Sheri laughed and swallowed the last of her tea. "I'll keep that in mind," she said as she set her mug down. "God, I've missed you."

"I've missed you, too," Kelli said, squeezing her hand. "And I'm especially glad your douchebag ex is gone." She frowned. "Was that too insensitive?"

"Please. I spent three years married to Captain Insensitive. At this point you could tell me to go fuck myself and I'd feel giddy someone's talking dirty to me."

"Is he still harassing you?"

Sheri shrugged. "I stopped answering his calls."

"Maybe you need a big, burly boyfriend around to scare him off. I could fix you up with someone."

"No way." Sheri shoved her mug away. "The last guy you tried to fix me up with asked me to starch his dress whites on the first date."

"Lesson learned. No more military men for you, I swear."

"No more *men,* period. Not right now."

Kelli shrugged. "Sooner or later, you need to get your mojo back. I stashed a box of super-magnum-jumbo condoms in your medicine cabinet for when the time comes. You're welcome."

"You're hopeless." Sheri grinned. "I promise I'll let you know when I'm ready to embrace my inner slut. In the meantime, I'm just glad to be here."

Kelli squeezed her hand. "I'm so happy you're finally on Kauai. This is a tough place to find a job, and it's even tougher to land a civilian gig at PMRF. Did you nail down your start date?"

Sheri nodded. "Monday morning. That's assuming the new nanny checks out. My brother insisted on hiring her, so we haven't even met yet. He's bringing her by in a few hours."

"Your brother? Which brother?" Kelli's face lit up with excitement and Sheri fought the urge to roll her eyes.

"MacArthur. Mac. You remember him from college?"

"I sure do. God, I had such a crush on him—"

"What if they love her more than me?" Sheri interrupted, not wanting Kelli to meander too far down the path of lusting after her commitment-phobic brother. "The twins, I mean. What if they love the nanny more?"

"Impossible. You've got great tits."

"Thank you. Exactly what every woman wants to be appreciated for."

"You know what I mean. For—uh—nursing and stuff. Not that your nanny won't have tits, but *yours* are dinner. You win."

"I'm bottle-feeding. And giving them soft foods from

a jar instead of organic pureed stuff I made myself. More things that make me a horrible mother."

"You're not a horrible mother. Knock that shit off or I'll put you in a headlock."

Sheri smiled, mostly because she knew Kelli wasn't kidding. Her friend might look dainty with her minuscule stature and a penchant for pastel sundresses, but Sheri had watched her wrestle a 160-pound pit bull to the floor of her vet clinic, and once saw her knock out a drunk frat boy with one punch when he tried to grab her ass.

Anyone who messed with Kelli lived to regret it.

The doorbell chimed, and Sheri jumped in her chair. In the back bedroom, both babies began to wail.

"Shit," she muttered, springing up from the table with a glance out the door at the big black sedan parked in her driveway. "Mac's early. You want to let them in, or calm the boys down?"

"A choice between ogling your hunky brother or getting pooped on. That's a tough call."

"Door!" Sheri ordered as the bell chimed again and the boys went on screaming. She ran for the twins' bedrooms and scooped up Jeffrey—or was it Jackson? No, definitely Jeffrey, though she had to check the back of his left thigh for the little birthmark to be sure. She cradled him in the crook of one arm, bouncing like a drunken kangaroo until his cries turned to soft whimpers. She laid him back down in his crib before leaning down to scoop up Jackson.

She wished she could still hold both of them at the same time. Maybe a bigger, more competent woman could. Hopefully the nanny was one of those hefty, matronly types with huge arms and the strength of a linebacker. Or maybe one of those earthy, crunchy women who could strap both babies into one of those complicated slings Sheri could never quite figure out.

"Shhhhh. Mommy's here," she whispered, bouncing the baby some more. She wasn't sure if the bouncing and declaration was comforting or more of an annoyance, but it was the best she had to offer.

"Hey Sher?" Kelli called from the living room. "You might want to come out here right away."

"Just a minute," she singsonged, trying to keep her voice light to avoid making the twins scream. "I'll be right there."

"You know that thing I said about the nanny's tits?" Kelli said, and Sheri turned to see her friend in the doorway with an odd expression on her face. "I don't think that's going to be an issue."

Kelli stepped aside like a magician revealing a rabbit behind a curtain. But there was no rabbit.

Instead, there was the biggest, burliest hunk of man flesh Sheri had laid eyes on since the day she and Kelli crashed a calendar shoot of shirtless Navy SEALs.

She swallowed hard, taking in the massive biceps, the chest that strained against a too-thin T-shirt, the ramrod posture she'd seen in every member of her military family dating back to the photos of Great-Great-Great-Grandpa Garrison in his Civil War uniform.

She swallowed again, wondering who'd sucked all the air from the room. Wondering, absurdly, if Kelli was joking about those condoms.

Chapter Two

Sam watched as the little blonde who'd led them through the house stepped farther into the bedroom and grinned at him and Mac. He stepped into the space behind her, conscious of the fact that he filled the whole doorframe.

Sheri stared at him, unblinking. Her feet were bare, and she wore knee-length sweatpants that looked like they'd been caught in a wood chipper. He couldn't tell if she was braless under her T-shirt or just very, very lush. She wore no makeup, and her chocolate curls were twisted into a sloppy topknot with something that looked like smushed carrot at the end of one ringlet.

He had never seen anything so beautiful.

"What the hell?" she asked.

Okay, so the admiration wasn't mutual.

Mac cleared his throat, and Sam stepped aside to let his pal through the door.

"Hey, Sher," Mac said, gathering his sister and the

whimpering baby into a gentle bear hug. "We caught an earlier connection out of Honolulu, so we got here sooner than expected. How are the little guys doing?"

Sheri pushed herself out of the hug and gave her brother a kiss on the cheek, then shifted the baby to one arm and slugged Mac hard in the shoulder. "It's good to see you, but you could have called, jerk!"

"And wake up the baby? Er, *babies*." Mac peered at one nephew, then the other. "God, they're getting big. Can I hold him?"

"Here, take Jackson. Er, Jeffrey. Whatever." She thrust the squirming infant into his arms, smiling at her brother despite the fact that she also looked like she might want to strangle him.

Mac pulled the baby against his chest as Sheri turned to pick up the other infant fussing in his crib. Sam took another step toward them and offered his best *trust me, I'm harmless* smile.

"May I?" he said, nodding toward the baby. "I have a nephew the same age. Seven months, right?"

Sheri stared at him like he'd suggested they take off their clothes and finger-paint rainbows on each other's chests, and he regretted his words instantly.

"I'm sorry, who are you?" Her tone wasn't angry, but it wasn't friendly, either.

Sam glanced at Mac, who was suddenly very interested in the top of his nephew's head. When Mac finally met his eyes, he wore the same expression he had when the two of them got busted stealing an opposing team's mascot in college.

Mac cleared his throat. "Sheri, you remember Sam Kercher?

Sam and I played football together in college. You two met at a party once."

"We did?" Sheri turned back to Sam, who forced himself not to move as she studied him. "Sorry, I don't remember. College was an awfully long time ago."

Sam wasn't sure whether to feel disappointed or pleased she didn't recall the dorky guy who face-planted into her cleavage and then attempted thirty seconds of awkward conversation that had clearly stuck a lot more firmly in his brain than hers.

Either way, one thing was pretty clear.

"So, uh, Mac didn't tell you about me?" he asked.

Sheri's brow crinkled and she turned to look at her brother. "Tell me what?"

Mac cleared his throat again and shifted the baby against his chest. "I've spent the last two weeks conducting a pretty intensive search for your nanny, Sher. I invested a lot of time and money in the process. I met with placement agencies, advertised the position, and interviewed qualified domestic help from around the world."

"Very thorough of you. What a loving brother," Kelli said, beaming at Mac like a puppy eyeing a hump-worthy shin.

"Obviously, you gave me your list of criteria," Mac continued. "Excellent cooking skills, good with children, experienced with diapering and childproofing a home, willing to do basic housekeeping, comfortable with a live-in position—"

"You can't be serious," she said, her face registering the fact that she'd caught on to what Mac was driving at. "You hired Beefcake here as my nanny?" She looked at Sam, then flushed. "No offense. I'm sure you're very nice."

"On occasion," Sam said, and took another step forward. "It's Sam, actually, but we can go with Mr. Beefcake if that's more comfortable."

She blinked at him. "Sam," she repeated. "Sammy the Nanny? You look more like a soldier. Or a lumberjack."

"I can assure you Sam is none of those things," Mac said. "He's a nanny. A very experienced nanny with all the qualifications you're seeking."

"I think the term is *manny*, actually," Kelli offered. "You know, a male nanny?"

Mac jostled the baby in his arms, though it was evident he had more need to soothe his sister. "It's a very common trend in families lacking a male role model—"

"There's no shortage of male role models in these kids' lives," Sheri snapped. "I have more brothers than pubic hairs, though right about now I'm thinking one less would be great." She froze as though replaying her last words in her mind and not liking the sound of them. "Less brothers, not—"

"There's an aesthetician in Princeville who does a great Brazilian bikini wax," Kelli offered, grinning. "I've got you covered there."

Sam was still reeling from the odd turn in conversation and from the fact that Mac clearly hadn't told Sheri anything about hiring him as her nanny. Maybe Mac was counting on her not being able to say no once he was in the house. A dirty trick, since she started her new job in a few days and wouldn't have time to find a nanny last-minute. Still, he felt lousy about it. Maybe this was a bad idea. Maybe he should leave. Maybe he should just thank them all for their time and—

"Shit, I think it just pooped," Mac said, and held the baby out in front of him like something contaminated, putting as much distance as possible between his chest and the squealing infant.

"Mac!" Sheri yelled, grabbing for her son. The jostling proved too much for the twin she already held, and he shrieked like he'd been stuck with a toothpick. Sheri stumbled as she tried to grab the baby from her brother's arms while still keeping her grip on the other.

Sam jumped. "Here, let me." He snatched the baby from Mac's arms and turned to Sheri. "Where are the diapers?"

She opened her mouth to say something, but he didn't wait. Spotting the changing table in the corner, he hustled the baby over and planted him on the cushioned surface. With one hand holding the little guy in place, he grabbed a baby wipe from the warmer, testing first to make sure the temperature was okay.

He'd watched his sisters do this a million times, and he'd downloaded a diapering tutorial that he'd watched on his laptop on the flight over.

You can do this, he commanded himself. *Think.*

The baby screeched with displeasure. He studied the squirming bundle and tried to remember the steps in the video.

Point the barrel in a safe direction and move the selector level to "safe" before pressing the magazine release button and—

Shit, no. Those were the steps for disassembling an M16 rifle.

Well, same idea, Sam thought as he stripped off the waterproof pants and the soggy cloth diaper, using one hand as a shield in case the little guy decided to demonstrate his aim. The diapering video he'd watched only dealt with the disposable kind, not these cloth things. He was way out of his league here, but maybe some of the steps were the same.

Pull the charging handle toward the rear of the rifle and press the bottom of the bolt catch—

Dammit, no. Something about safety pins or lotion maybe?

He held the little guy in place with one hand as he grabbed a clean diaper and some pins from the basket beside him. Frowning in concentration, he cleaned off the baby, trying not to gag as he reminded himself he'd seen worse things in military mess halls.

Unthread the sling from the metal loops on the buttstock and barrel to remove the sling from the rifle.

No, no! Goddammit, *concentrate.* Or maybe those really were the right instructions? He ankle-lifted the baby and slid the fresh diaper under him, then got to work folding and fastening.

He stabbed himself with a diaper pin but didn't flinch, even when he saw blood welling on the tip of his thumb. He grabbed another diaper wipe and surreptitiously swiped the digit before fastening the last pin in place.

He surveyed his work, nodding once. Not bad. Not bad at all. He'd once set a platoon record for speed of rifle assembly. This wasn't so different, and he hadn't gotten shot in the face.

"There you go, little guy," Sam said gently patting the baby's bare belly. "Nice job."

The baby gave him a toothless grin and gurgled. He grinned back and scooped the baby in his arms, turning to face his audience.

Everyone stared, no one uttering a sound. Sheri had put the other baby back in his crib at some point, so he stepped forward and placed the fresh-smelling infant in her arms.

"Here you go," he said, feeling stupidly dizzy as his forearm brushed her breast. "Good as new."

She blinked at him, then looked down at the baby. When she looked back at Sam, he felt his heart flip over in his chest.

"Thank you," she said.

"No problem," he said, wondering how he could possibly feel so electrified by her with his hands covered in baby lotion and his shirt reeking of reprocessed Gerber.

He picked up the soiled diaper from the changing table and handed it to Mac without tearing his eyes off Sheri. Mac grunted in protest, but took the diaper anyway.

Sheri smiled at Sam. "When can you start?"

• • •

Five years ago, my idea of sexy was a guy who picked up the tab for my tequila shots while I danced on the table with my girlfriends, Sheri thought. *Now I'm ready to throw my panties at a guy who knows which end of the baby to put the diaper on?*

She shook her head. "I really need to get out more."

"What?" Sam asked, and Sheri was startled to realize she'd spoken aloud. Again. She opened her mouth to give an explanation, but Kelli beat her to it.

"She talks to herself a lot these days," Kelli offered. "But she says a lot of good stuff, so pay attention." Kelli squeezed her hand and grinned. "You're right, Sher. You *should* get out. You're starting a new job Monday, and if you're planning to wear any of those things we unpacked last week, I'm going to set fire to your closet right now."

Sheri sighed. "I have clothes."

True, she'd been avoiding trying most of them on or stepping on a scale to see if she was anywhere near her pre-pregnancy weight, but surely she had *something* that would fit right.

"Even if you don't want new clothes for work, you'll need them when you start dating," Kelli pointed out. "Remember what I said about getting your mojo back?"

"I need a boyfriend like I need a toenail fungus."

"You'll be ready sooner or later," Kelli said. "And at least here on Kauai, your odds are better of finding someone who's not an overbearing military jerk like your ex." She flashed a grin at Mac. "No offense."

"None taken."

"I'm not dating," Sheri said. "Not military men, not chest-thumping alpha males, and definitely not two-faced, dishonest bastards who pretend to be honorable when they're lying to your face."

Sam coughed, and Sheri turned to look at him. "You're not getting sick, are you?"

"No," he said, a little red-faced. "No, of course not. Fit as a fiddle."

"I see," she said, trying not to notice his biceps or chest or any other fit body parts.

Mac caught her eye and gave her a stern look. She resisted the urge to stick her tongue out at him like she might have in high school when he warned her away from dating his buddies. She had plenty of her own reasons for not getting bowled over by the force of her own hormones.

Still, a girl could look —

"Come on," Kelli said, grabbing her arm. "These two muscleheads can watch the twins. Macy's is having a sale, so we can head to Lihue and get a manicure while we're at it. Maybe even a haircut. You want to look good on your first day, right?"

Sheri hesitated, looked down at the gurgling baby in her arms. She was pretty sure *normal mothers* didn't leave their babies with strange men they'd only known five minutes. She bit her lip and looked back at Mac, and then at Sam, who gave her a reassuring smile.

"Consider it a trial run," he said, his voice low and soft. "A job interview of sorts. Besides, Mac will be here to make sure I take great care of your little guys."

She snorted. "I'm not sure the guy who just bypassed the diaper pail and put the dirty diaper in a basket of clean laundry is the best one to look to for adult supervision," Sheri said. "But thank you. I accept. I haven't been out of the house for a week, and I need to grab groceries anyway."

"Already handled," Sam said. "We passed Costco on the way from the airport, so we stopped off and grabbed a few things. Milk, eggs, bread, apples, wine — "

"Ohmygod, I love you," Kelli said. "If you don't get to be her manny, will you be mine?"

He smiled politely. "How many children do you have?"

"None. That's not a problem, is it?"

Sam laughed and turned back to Sheri. He folded his arms over his chest, and she resisted the urge to gawk at the most impressive set of biceps she'd ever seen. His eyes were icy blue, and his rumpled hair curled warm and golden brown at the nape of his neck — a little too long, which shouldn't have been a turn-on, but after so many years of men with military buzz cuts, she ached to run her fingers through it. He wore a faded surfer T-shirt and a pair of wrinkled khaki shorts that looked soft from too many washings. She had the absurd urge to rub her cheek on them.

"I'm sorry to show up unexpectedly like this," Sam said. "I'll beat up MacArthur if you want."

She smiled and smoothed her hands down the front of her T-shirt, feeling oddly self-conscious. "That won't be necessary," she said. "Kelli will handle him."

"My pleasure," Kelli agreed, shooting a look of lust at Mac.

He didn't appear to notice.

"It *was* a bit of a shock expecting Mary Poppins and seeing Arnold Schwarzenegger," Sheri admitted. "If you don't mind, I need a little time to think things over."

"Absolutely," he said. "Go run your errands, and I'll hold down the fort with Mac. We'll have dinner ready when you get back. How do you feel about chicken cordon bleu?"

"For—uh, dinner?" she stammered, too dumbfounded to even remember what chicken cordon bleu was, let alone whether she liked it.

"No, for breakfast, dork," Mac said, giving his sister a squeeze as he took the baby out of her arms and a gentle push toward the door. "Of course for dinner. Sam's a great cook. One of many reasons I *wisely* hired him as your nanny. I guarantee after one mouthful, you'll be begging for more."

She swallowed and nodded, darting another glance at Sam.

"I don't doubt it," she said, and hurried out the door.

Chapter Three

Sheri wasn't sure which felt more amazing—shopping with a girlfriend sans screaming infants and a heavy diaper bag, or returning to a house that smelled like a five-star restaurant exploded in a glorious cloud of yum.

"That was so good," Kelli gasped as she set down her fork after a final bite of chicken. "Where'd you learn to cook like that?"

Sam opened his mouth to say something, but Mac beat him to it.

"Sam's very modest about his culinary training," he said. "He's clearly quite skilled though. More wine?"

Sheri hesitated, then held out her glass. "Just a tiny bit. It's very good. I haven't had wine in ages."

"Sam picked it out," Mac said, nearly filling her glass to the brim. She gazed longingly at it, knowing she should probably protest, but enjoying the idea of an adult meal so much she nearly swooned.

"At least let me give you money for the wine," Sheri said as Sam stood and began gathering plates. "Please, it's the least I can do."

"No need," he said as he picked up her empty salad bowl. A fork clattered against a knife, and Sam stole a quick glance at the baby monitor before picking up Kelli's empty plate. "Besides, Mac paid for everything. I just picked it out."

"It's part of the deal, Sheri," Mac said before she could argue. "You put me in charge of hiring your nanny, so I pay for everything. Food included. Sam works for me now, so he's got an expense account to cover anything he might require to care for you and the twins."

"But that's ridiculous," Sheri protested. "I only asked you for help *looking* for a nanny. Not to hire me a goddamn linebacker and fund the whole thing."

"I'm an overachiever," Mac said. He took a final sip of wine and stood up. "Speaking of which, duty calls. I have to take care of some business, and I might be out pretty late. You'll see that Sam either gets back to the hotel or settled into that room you set up for a nanny?"

Sheri frowned. "Mac, we need to talk about—"

"Bye, Sher," he said, cutting her off with a hasty kiss on the cheek before he marched out the door.

She looked at Sam, who was scraping a plate over the garbage disposal. He looked huge and imposing in her tiny kitchen, but it was clear he felt comfortable there, and he obviously knew what he was doing.

Beside Sheri, Kelli stood up.

"I have to run, too, but call me if you need someone to watch the boys sleep while you run Sam to the hotel." She lowered her voice to a conspiratorial whisper. "Or you could just have him stay here. You've got the nanny room all set up, or there's plenty of space in your bed—"

"Good night, Kel," Sheri said a little too loudly.

Kelli giggled, leaning closer to whisper again. "He looks like the sort of guy who'd be very attentive to your orgasm."

Sheri felt her cheeks flame, and she pinched Kelli on the thigh before stealing a look at him. He was intent on scrubbing the corners of her sink with a Brillo pad, and didn't seem to have heard Kelli's pronouncement.

"You can't tell that sort of thing at a glance," Sheri whispered.

"Sure I can. I had one just looking at him." She stood up and dodged out of the way before Sheri could swat her.

Turning back to Sam, Kelli eyed him up and down one more time. "Good to meet you, Big Guy."

He nodded. "Ma'am. Very nice meeting you."

"Christ, you make me sound like a schoolteacher or a drill sergeant or something. Please, just call me Kelli."

"Nice to meet you, Kelli," Sam repeated, frowning a little as he turned back to his dishes.

"Thank you for dragging me out shopping," Sheri said as Kelli grabbed her purse and headed for the door. "Seriously, if it weren't for you, I'd go to my first day of work wearing yoga pants."

"We'll have to do it again sometime. Have a great night, guys!"

And with that, Sheri found herself alone with her new manny.

Well, technically, she still hadn't made up her mind about that. She watched Sam for a moment, his massive shoulders bent over the kitchen sink as he scrubbed a baking sheet with a fierceness that made his forearms ripple. A splash of soapy dishwater hit the front of his shirt, and she admired the outline of his perfect washboard abs through the damp cotton. His fingers flexed around the sudsy sponge as he slid it over the slick pan.

Sheri cleared her throat. "Thank you for dinner. It was incredible. The salad was delicious."

He nodded and looked up from the sink. "There was a good farmers' market just up the road. Great fresh produce."

"Right," she said, thinking *normal mothers* probably knew the location of every farmers' market on the island so they never ran out of nutritious, organic vegetables to steam and puree for their little angels. She stood up as he returned to the table to grab the empty wineglasses.

"Please," she said. "At least let me finish the dishes. You've done so much already."

"No way," he said, planting a firm hand on her shoulder and pushing her back into her chair. His hand lingered there for a few beats and Sheri shivered from the heat of his fingers and the delicious pressure of his palm cupping her shoulder.

God, how long had it been since a man touched her? Maybe Kelli was right about this mojo thing.

He hesitated, then drew his hand back and smiled, making Sheri thankful he couldn't read her thoughts.

"Really, I've got it," he insisted. "Just let me help you. Can I get you another glass of wine?"

"I'm fine, thank you. Look, I think we should talk."

"Okay."

She cleared her throat again, not sure why she felt so nervous. "I won't pretend I wasn't shocked to have you just show up here with Mac informing me you're the new nanny.

But you do seem to know your way around a changing table and a kitchen, and right now I'm not in a position to be picky."

He raised one eyebrow. "That's your idea of a vote of confidence?"

"Sorry. I'm new at this."

He grinned, and she felt bad for antagonizing him. Hell, he'd just cooked her dinner. She'd given a blow job to the last guy who'd done that, and she hadn't even liked him much. Okay, so he'd been her husband, but really—

"Do you mind if I ask you a few questions?" she asked, eager to shift her brain from that train of thought. "I know Mac already interviewed you, but I'd feel better if I got to know a little more about you and your qualifications before we commit to anything."

"Fire away."

She thought about it for a moment, wondering what sort of questions *normal moms* would ask their potential nannies. Something about feeding times and care plans and childrearing philosophies?

"So, um, how'd you get started as a—as a *manny*?"

He dried the baking sheet with a turquoise towel, then bent down to tuck the pan in the drawer beneath the oven. Sheri was so distracted staring at his ass that she forgot she'd asked a question.

"I have six older sisters," he said as he stood up and set the dish towel on the counter, anchoring his hands on either side of it. "Five of them are married with kids, which means I have a whopping total of six nieces, eight nephews, and two more on the way."

"Wow," she said, taken aback. "You must have a close

family?"

"You could say that. My mom died when I was five, and my dad didn't marry my stepmom for another fifteen years. My sisters sort of took over mothering me, while my dad did his best to make sure I didn't go to school wearing their doll clothes and an apron."

She laughed, trying to picture a smaller, less-buff version of Sam in a pink frilly apron. Her brain took another detour from there, conjuring up images of current-day Sam wearing nothing but a smile and a barbecue apron, the strings cinched loosely above that tight, curved backside and—

"Wh—where did you do your culinary training?" she asked, tripping over her tongue.

He wiped his hands on the dish towel and hung it neatly on a hook before leaning against the counter and looking at her with those piercing blue eyes. "I spent a lot of time training overseas," he said. "Gonsalves in Japan, Sigonella in Italy."

"Wow, that sounds exotic." She wasn't sure if those were cities or restaurants or cooking schools, but figured it didn't matter. The guy obviously knew which side of a pan to grease.

"So tell me a little bit about the last family you worked with," she continued. "What was that experience like?"

He scratched his jaw, drawing her eyes to the faint dusting of stubble and the tiny scar running just below his left ear. She wondered what it would feel like to trace her finger over it, to touch the tip of her tongue—

"It was noisy," he said. "Chaotic. Messy. Sometimes heartwarming and sometimes heartbreaking. There were times I thought I wouldn't survive the night, and other times

I kinda wished I wouldn't, but I'm very proud of the work I did. Of my time there."

She smiled. "Sounds like you've got a pretty good handle on living with small children."

She watched his Adam's apple bob as he swallowed. "You could say that."

"So why did you leave your last position?"

He hesitated—so infinitesimally, Sheri thought she might have imagined it. Or maybe he just remembered he needed to put soap in the dishwasher, since that's what he turned to do. "It was time to move on," he said at last, clicking the door shut and flipping the switch to set the appliance humming. "Look, I know Mac did a thorough background check, and I'm sure he'd be happy to give you copies of my references and—"

"No, that won't be necessary," she said, feeling a little foolish. "I just wanted to know a little more about you, that's all. My brother might be a domineering jerk sometimes, but if he says he's known you for years and he vouches for your qualifications, that's good enough for me. He'd do anything to make sure the twins and I are well cared for."

"Very true," Sam said, nodding. He pressed his palms against the counter again, then moved out from behind it to stand in front, less than two feet from where Sheri sat. She could feel the heat from the bare skin of his legs, and she wondered what it would feel like to run her fingers up those thick, muscular calves.

"Do you mind if I ask you a few questions?" he asked.

"By all means," she said, drawing her eyes from his legs to his face. "I guess if you might be living here, it's only fair that you know more about us."

"The twins' father—is he in the picture?"

Sheri gripped the edge of the table, surprised he hadn't started with a softball question about nap schedules or immunization records.

"Jonathan is…well, I'm not entirely certain. He's PCSing—um, that's military-speak for permanent change of station—but I'm not sure where his new command will be. He hasn't told me, and I haven't asked."

"So he's in limbo?"

"Something like that. Usually he has a few weeks between an old command and a new one, so he's probably in Hawaii somewhere. Things are still pretty new with the divorce and everything, so we're not really communicating that well." She wished she'd agreed to that glass of wine after all.

"Does he contact you?"

"Sometimes." Sheri glanced down at her hands, not sure she wanted to reveal how often Jonathan had been calling. She wasn't afraid of him—not really—but she didn't like talking to him. Especially when he started making noise about getting back together, about being a family again.

She shuddered at the thought.

"Sorry, I didn't mean to pry," he said. "I only wondered how involved he is and whether he'll be okay with the boys having a nanny. Some guys might be uncomfortable with the idea of another man watching his children. Looking after his wife."

"Ex-wife," she snapped a little too gruffly. "That lying, cheating asshole lost the privilege of calling me his wife the second he stuck his dick in another woman."

"Right. Sorry."

She shook her head. "No, I'm sorry. I didn't mean to yell. I just hate lying. Lying is the absolute worst thing. Worse than riptides and parking tickets and pubic lice combined."

"Of course." There was a flicker of something in his eyes—amusement? Embarrassment? It was gone in an instant, whatever it was.

"Anyway," she said, hoping to steer the conversation back on track, "the divorce has only been final a month, but the marriage ended the second he walked out the door."

Sam nodded, his eyes locked on hers. She looked away, glancing down at the French manicure Kelli had insisted would make her look sophisticated and stylish. When she looked up, he was still watching her.

"He's an idiot," Sam said, his blue eyes fiery in the dim light of the kitchen. "Your ex-husband."

"Yes," she agreed, shivering a little under the heat of his gaze.

"He didn't deserve you."

"I know. He also gave up the right to have any say in who watches the children or who lives in my house when he left us for a tramp with neon hot pants and gravity-defying fake boobs," she said.

He snorted. "Trust me, sweetheart. Fake tits have nothing on your incredible, natural—" He froze, then cleared his throat. "More wine?"

"You already asked me that." She fought the urge to smile as he tore his eyes from her chest and began scrubbing the counter with a vengeance. She should probably be offended, but she was too damn flattered to muster any real indignation.

"Sorry," he said. "That was inappropriate."

"Not a problem." Sheri tried to ignore the warm, tingly feeling pulsing through her body as he looked at her again. His eyes swept over her breasts, down the curve of her hip. She straightened a little, startled to realize she wanted him to look.

"I haven't spoken with my ex recently," she said to diffuse the tension warming the room. "We handled most of the divorce settlements and custody arrangements through lawyers. It got pretty ugly."

"Was he abusive?"

She shook her head. "Verbally, I guess. Look, I have full custody, so any decisions concerning Jeffrey and Jackson's well-being are mine to make."

Sam nodded. "Fair enough. I'm—uh—I'm sorry for your loss."

She released her grip on the table and laughed. "I like the way you make him sound dead instead of like a deadbeat. I actually might've preferred that." She stood up, ready to be finished with this line of questioning. "Okay, why don't we give this a trial run with the manny thing?"

"You're sure?"

She nodded. "We can give it a couple weeks and see how that goes. You seem like a good guy, and it's obvious my brother did his due diligence in hiring you. Sounds like he already handled the salary and benefits and everything. Are you okay with those arrangements?"

"Mac was very generous."

"I imagine so. He's mysterious as hell, and I have no idea what he does for a living, but he's richer than God and takes good care of his family. Are you—I mean, are you comfortable working here? Do you think the position is a good fit?"

He gave her a smile that made her belly twist pleasantly. "I think we'll both find the arrangement mutually satisfying."

"Good. That's good." She stood up and started down the hall, conscious of Sam following closely behind her. "Well, I'll show you the room I'd prepared for the nanny. I hope you're okay with apricot walls and pastel yellow sheets. I decorated before I knew you'd be more Bruce Willis in *Die Hard* than Maria from *Sound of Music*."

"I can try to remember some of the words to 'My Favorite Things' if that helps," he said, grinning. "Wasn't there something about raindrops on roses, whiskers on kittens—"

She laughed and halted in the doorway of his room. "Here we are. If it makes you feel better, the sheets are very high thread count, so they'll be soft and luxurious on your skin." She swallowed, feeling like an idiot as she imagined his big, warm body sliding between the cool sheets, his thick legs twining with hers, his arm slung across her breasts as he pulled her close and—

"Air-conditioning," she squeaked, striding across the room to grab the remote control. "Use this to change the temperature if you get too hot, or you can opt for the ceiling fan and open windows like I do."

"I'll be fine," he said, his massive hand closing around hers as he accepted the device and smiled. "Thank you."

She nodded and tried to smile back, but her heart was slamming hard against her rib cage and her whole body ached with the need to feel those massive palms moving over her body.

"Okay then," she said, stepping back and reluctantly pulling her hand from his. "Let me know if you need anything."

He looked at her, and Sheri felt her stomach do a big, swirly flip in her abdomen. He held her gaze, his blue eyes boring into hers. Even if she'd wanted to look away, she was frozen in place. Her face felt hot, her toes felt cold, and somewhere in the middle she felt deliciously warm like she'd just swallowed a quart of melted butter.

"If I need anything," he murmured, "you'll be the first to know."

Chapter Four

For two hours, Sam lay awake staring at his apricot walls and listening to the chirp of crickets and the occasional crow of a rooster who had no sense of time. On the shelf beside the bed, the baby monitor offered the soft swish of hushed breathing.

He thought about Sheri sleeping soundly in the next room, just on the other side of the wall. He imagined her lying tangled in the sheets with all that curly hair spilling across the pillow and her nipples puckered from the air-conditioning. His heart clenched. What did she wear to bed? Was it silky and soft, or did she skip nightwear altogether in deference to the Hawaii heat?

He rolled over and tried to refocus his brain on the job he'd come to do. Mac's sources had confirmed that Jonathan Price had returned to Hawaii, but he was all the way over in Honolulu.

For now.

He was glad Sheri made no mention of her ex trying to contact her, but he needed to be on high alert. For the next two weeks, Lieutenant Limpdick could show up at any time. Sam needed to be ready.

After Sheri had gone to bed, he'd done a thorough scan of the house. He'd found no trace of broken locks on windows or doors, though it was clear she could be lax about remembering to lock up. He made a mental note to be extra vigilant there. He'd found no unsecured guns or electrical outlets without child protectors. Nothing more threatening than a personal massager with a slightly frayed cord tucked behind her nightstand.

He tried not to dwell too much on that image, rolling over again and commanding his mind to go somewhere else.

He hated sneaking around and lying, especially after what she'd said earlier.

Lying is the absolute worst thing. Worse than riptides and parking tickets and pubic lice combined.

The least he could do was keep the lies to a minimum. Okay, so the chicken cordon bleu had come from a box at Costco. Gonsalves wasn't a Japanese culinary school, but the Jungle Warfare Training Center in Okinawa where he'd been as a young Marine. And he'd done a few shifts in the mess hall, just like he had on the base in Sigonella in Italy.

And he'd told the truth about the emotional impacts of his last job, even if he'd been vague on specifics.

He closed his eyes again, but opened them quickly when he saw the face. A boy no more than ten years old looking up at the birds. Or at something else overhead, Sam still wondered. The boy's eyes flashed with fear or determination—which had it been?

Just a boy—

"Enough," he said out loud, and sat up in bed. He smoothed his hands through his hair, then lay back down, flipping over to his other side and searching for a cool spot on the sheets.

He punched his pillow and didn't sleep.

• • •

The next morning, Sam got up early. It was an old habit from years of early drills in the Marines. He hopped out of bed, eager to get started on the day. Breakfast he could handle. He might not be the best cook in the world, but he knew how to make bacon and eggs without burning down a house.

He made his bed with perfect hospital corners, remembering the sergeant who insisted on bouncing a quarter off the recruits' tightly tucked sheets. He frowned at his handiwork, recalling what Mac said about masking his rigid inner Marine. Sam bent down and untucked one of the corners, pausing to rumple the quilt before doing the same to his own hair. He thought about shaving, but decided to skip it. The rumpled look was part of his disguise.

Within twenty minutes, he had bacon sizzling on the stove. The babies were awake when he checked, so he changed them both and set them in their little bouncy chairs to watch him work. Instead of sitting quiet and smiley like babies in a diaper commercial, they took turns shrieking and banging their little plastic stacking cups against each other.

"Shhh, keep it down," he murmured. "You don't want to wake up your mom."

The babies looked at him and shrieked louder, one of

them blowing a big snot bubble his brother tried to grab. Sam turned around to focus on mixing a pitcher of orange juice from a can, wondering if he could convince Sheri it was freshly squeezed.

No. Keep the lies minimal. Keep things simple.

"Morning," Sheri said, and Sam spun around.

Her hair was in loose ringlets around her shoulders and she definitely wasn't wearing a bra under her thin cami top. She looked sleepy and disheveled and so deliciously fuckable, Sam dropped his spatula.

"M-morning," he stammered back, stooping to pick up the spatula and tossing it in the sink. He grabbed a clean one from the holder beside the stove, and used it to flip the bacon.

She slid her fingers through her curls, and he ached to know what it felt like to have all those ringlets twisting around his hand.

"You don't have to do that," she said, yawning a little as she shifted from one bare foot to the other. "On days I'm not working, you aren't obligated to—"

"You want one egg or two?"

She blinked, then nodded. "Two, please."

"Mac said you like 'em over easy. That still the case?"

"Yes, thank you. That would be wonderful. Can I at least make you some coffee?"

"I don't drink coffee, but there's a pot brewing right now."

"Christ, did you paint my house, too?"

He grinned. "That's next week."

He set the plate down in front of her, then strode to the fridge to pull out a pair of gummy teething rings.

"Here you go, guys," he said, handing each twin a chilled ring. Blessedly, they stopped shrieking, and Sam felt a surge of pride at his own dumb luck. He smiled at her. "My sisters' kids loved these things."

Jeffrey and Jackson stuffed the goo-filled rings in their mouths, drool running onto their bibs. Sam watched with relief as they gummed the toys with enthusiastic glee.

He grabbed his own plate and sat down beside Sheri. "I hope it's okay that I already fed them. They were up early, and I didn't want to wake you. The guidelines you wrote up were really helpful."

"Good," she said, picking up her toast and taking a bite. "I didn't want to flood you with information, but I tried to be thorough. Sorry, I guess some of it doesn't apply to you. I wrote that whole thing when I expected someone a little different as a nanny."

"Not a problem. The section on the best places for manicures and the discount coupon for the bikini shop should be helpful."

She laughed and took a bite of eggs. "Speaking of bikinis, I was going to take the boys to the beach today. You're welcome to come along, get the lay of the land a bit."

His brain got so hung up on the words "bikini" and "lay," he almost didn't register the rest of what she said. "The beach?"

"Probably Poipu. I have a little tent I set up to keep the sun off their skin, and it's a nice day to get outside and relax a little. My schedule's going to be nutty after I start the new job, so I figure it's my last chance to lie in the sand and read a book and splash around a little with the boys. You don't have to go if you don't want to. I just thought—"

"I'll go," he said, a little too quickly. "I wanted to check out the area. I've never spent time on Kauai."

"It's a lot different from Oahu. That's where my ex-husband was stationed the last couple years. Kauai is much smaller, more lush and green and scenic, without as many people."

"Think you'll ever return to the mainland?"

She shrugged and shoveled up the last forkful of eggs. "I was planning to move to Oregon or maybe California after Jonathan left. I have a lot of friends there. But then I got this job with the Pacific Missile Range Facility, and it's pretty much my dream job. I couldn't leave. Besides, my father's a general stationed in Honolulu, so this way they get to see their grandkids on occasion."

"That's nice."

"Sometimes. Sometimes I wonder what the hell I was thinking."

She didn't specify what she was referring to, and Sam was so fixated on watching her lick egg yolk off the back of her fork that he didn't think to ask.

She used her toast to scrape up the last of her eggs before standing and clearing her plate.

"I'll finish up the dishes and then take a quick shower before I throw a few things in a beach bag," she said. "Think you'll be ready in thirty minutes?"

"Absolutely," he said, tearing his eyes off her mouth.

Thirty minutes turned out to be more like an hour and thirty minutes, not that Sam was complaining. He liked watching her bustling around the house, hunting for the boys' sun hats and smearing their little bodies with sunscreen that made them glow like mutant pink slugs. He tried to help, but she nudged him aside.

"This is what *normal mothers* do," she'd said, so he gave up and went outside.

He picked up the newspaper in the driveway, glancing at the headlines before setting it on the rickety little table just inside the front door. Figuring he had time to kill, he walked back out into the sunshine, studying Sheri's car.

It was a late-model sedan, nothing fancy, nothing to attract attention. The bases of the twins' car seats were buckled into the backseat, looking secure and tidy in spite of the kid gunk streaked on one of them below where the carrier would latch into place. He studied the apparatus carefully, assessing how to operate it.

He peered through each window, taking inventory. Sheri's sunglasses were tucked into the cup holder, and a small white shopping bag sat on the floorboard of the passenger side. He shielded his eyes, scoping out the safety features, making sure everything looked okay.

Satisfied with the car's interior, he dropped to the ground beside it and peered underneath. Everything looked pretty good. A little corrosion on the undercarriage, but no ticking bombs or loose wires or anything.

For crying out loud, he chided himself. *You're performing a bomb sweep in a Hawaiian suburb? Get off the ground and start acting like a manny instead of a Marine.*

"What are you doing?" Sheri called, and he sat up so fast he smacked his head on the undercarriage. He crawled out from under the car, trying to look nonchalant.

"Thought I saw a little oil on your driveway," he said as he got to his feet. "Just wanted to check for leaks."

She smiled and pushed a double stroller toward him.

The boys' carriers were latched into place on it, and Sam marveled at the technology that created such an apparatus. He'd seen tanks less cleverly designed.

He looked at Sheri, marveling even more at how she was designed. How flawlessly beautiful she was. She was dressed simply in khaki shorts and a blue T-shirt that matched the straps on her flip-flops. Her eyes sparkled in the midmorning sun, and her hair was piled in a topknot he wanted to tug free just to watch the curls tumble over her shoulders.

"So you're a manny mechanic?" she teased.

"Nah, it's just a male requirement to crawl around under automobiles every now and then and grunt a few times. They take away our jockstraps if we don't do it."

She laughed, a sweet, warm sound that reminded him of calypso music. As she reached the car, Sheri flipped the button to unlock the doors, then popped one open. She clicked Jackson's carrier off the stroller and latched it into place on the base in the backseat. Sam watched closely, then followed suit with Jeffrey, patting his warm, squirmy body to make sure he was secure.

"All set?" he asked.

"At least until we get two blocks away and I realize I forgot my water bottle. Or my sunglasses. Or my book. Or my cooler. That's kinda my thing." She smiled, and Sam felt his gut turn to melted chocolate.

The drive to Poipu beach was lovely, with tree tunnels and lush fields rolling past in a blur of green and blue. "Right here is the turnoff," Sheri said as she turned the car onto a narrow side street and continued toward a large parking area. "It's easy to miss if you don't know where you're going."

"Right," he said, and hopped out of the car to unbuckle

the babies. Loaded down like pack mules, he and Sheri made the slow trudge across the sand. He let her lead the way, already conjuring up a delicate way to redirect her if she chose a spot that left them with too many people at their backs or no easy escape routes. Instead, she picked a quiet stretch of sand backed up against a low hedge near a footpath leading to an outdoor shower. Two potential escape routes.

There's nothing to escape from. You're on a beach, not a battlefield.

Sam relaxed and began setting up the canopy. He thought about removing his shirt, but decided against it. His right shoulder blade bore an elaborate tattoo of a bulldog—a devil dog, or teufelshunde as the German soldiers had dubbed the US Marines in the Battle of Belleau Wood in 1918.

The design was pretty generic, and didn't reference the Marines or "Semper fi." Still, Sheri came from a military family. He couldn't risk her recognizing the significance of the symbol.

"I hope you put on sunscreen," Sheri said. "It might not feel that warm, but you'll burn fast even on a day like today."

Sam nodded, keeping one eye on the beach. "Better safe than sorry," he said.

His eyes swept the sand, looking for threats, looking for anything out of the ordinary.

Stop it. It's just a goddamn beach.

But he couldn't do it. He went back to studying his surroundings, cataloging every piece of driftwood, every stranger around him. At the edge of the shoreline, a young Hispanic couple with matching infinity tattoos on their wrists clasped hands and splashed into the waves. To the right, a bald guy fought to don his snorkel mask and swim fins, looking like an overcooked sea creature. To the left, a small crowd gathered around a makeshift barricade marking a sandy strip where a large sea turtle had crawled ashore to snooze in the sun. Sam breathed in the scent of sunscreen and ocean air, watching for anything out of the ordinary.

Suddenly, he saw it. A man walking alone with a bulging duffel bag slung over his right shoulder. He wore a hat with the brim pulled low, hiding his face. Something long and solid poked through the duffel.

Sam froze, every muscle in his body tense. Behind him, Sheri fussed with the twins, kneeling in the sand to offer juice cups and kisses. He reached instinctively for the pistol strapped to his shoulder holster.

Shit.

He'd locked his gun in a desk drawer back at the house, knowing a holster might raise questions on a beach outing with two infants and a woman who had no idea he was anything other than the football-playing manny he claimed to be. He studied the man walking toward them and memorized his gait, the suspicious duffel, the averted gaze. Sam stared, unblinking.

The guy was getting closer, and Sam moved into position, putting his body between the man and Sheri. A glint of metal flashed at the edge of the duffel, and he watched the guy's hand drop as he reached for it.

Slowly, the man brought his hand up. Sam's heart leaped to his throat as he recognized the cold steel, the familiar shape of the rifle, the sudden burst of adrenaline in his own veins.

"No!" Sam yelled, and dove for Sheri.

Chapter Five

The feel of Sam's massive, muscled frame pressing her into the sand was so foreign, so unexpected, so deliciously welcome, that it took Sheri a few beats to ask the obvious question.

"Um, Sam?"

"Yeah?"

"Is there a reason you just tackled me?"

He sat up and straightened his dark sunglasses, pausing to brush sand off her arm as he scowled down the beach at an old man sweeping a metal detector along the edge of the water. She watched him stare at the guy for a few beats before he turned back to her.

"Sorry about that," he said, brushing more sand off her shoulder. "I thought you were headed for the water, and I had to stop you. It hasn't been very long since you ate breakfast, and I don't want you to get leg cramps and drown."

She struggled to sit up, feeling oddly disappointed not to have his body pressed against hers anymore. Was she out of her mind? Was he?

"You're nuts," she said at last. "But thank you. I guess. You know that's an old wives' tale, right?"

"What's that?" he asked, still watching the guy with the metal detector.

"That thing they used to tell kids about how they shouldn't go in the water after eating or they'll get cramps and drown. I looked it up on Snopes.com once when I was researching all these things I needed to prepare for in raising two boys so close to the beach, and I learned that's not true. Doctors say that doesn't really happen."

"Huh," he said. "Sorry. Here, let me help you up."

He jumped to his feet, surprisingly graceful for such a big guy. He reached down and hoisted her to her feet, dusting more sand off her elbow, her stomach, her hip, the back pocket of her shorts. As his hand made contact with her backside through the thin fabric of her shorts, she gasped and pressed against him ever so slightly, craving more.

"Sorry about that," he said, dropping his hands to his sides and looking a bit like a naughty schoolboy. "Just being thorough."

"I appreciate it," she said, wishing she'd managed to cover her whole body in sand like a cinnamon-sugar doughnut so he could spend the whole day dusting her off. "So you must've been a defensive lineman?"

"What?"

"When you played football with Mac. That was quite a tackle you just pulled." She smiled to show she was teasing, but he looked mildly horrified.

"Right," he said. "Turn around." He maneuvered her the other way and dusted some more sand off her right thigh. She shivered and glanced back at the little canopy where Jeffrey and Jackson slept like the dead.

"Wow, the boys conked out fast," she said. "I expected them to be amped up about the water and sand and birds. Maybe they're still too young for this."

A *normal mother* would have known that. Would have instinctively realized the appropriate age to bring small children to the beach with visions of making sand castles and gleefully tossing Cheerios to birds on the beach. Clearly, she had a lot to learn.

"You okay?" Sam asked.

She turned back to him. Even behind his dark sunglasses, she could tell he was studying her. "I'm fine."

"I didn't hurt you, did I?"

"No, why?"

"You had a funny look on your face just then."

Sheri sighed. "Have you ever worried you're not cut out for the job you thought you were destined to do?"

She expected him to laugh or shore her up with encouraging platitudes, but instead, he nodded. "Plenty of times."

"How did you handle it?"

"Not as well as I could have."

She nodded, surprised by his frank answer. "I have a confession."

"Oh?"

"I'm switching back to disposable diapers."

He raised an eyebrow. "That's your idea of a confession? I thought you were going to tell me you club baby seals."

She smiled and gave a little shrug. "Ask my Mommy and

Me group which is worse and I think they'd say the diapers."

"You need new friends."

"Maybe. I'm still new in town, so maybe I'll find a mothers' group that enjoys seal clubbing." She reached across him for her beach tote, and felt his whole body tense as her breast brushed his arm through her T-shirt. "I guess now's the best time to read, huh? While the boys are sleeping."

She pulled a romance novel out of her bag and rested it on the corner of her beach towel. She hesitated, glancing at Sam. "This is my first time in public in a bathing suit since they were born."

"Would you like me to—uh—avert my eyes?"

She laughed. "Not unless you want to. I won't take offense either way. Two good things about going through a lousy divorce right after giving birth? Stress melts off a lot of the baby weight," she said, tugging her T-shirt over head. "And discovering there are tougher things in life than a few extra pounds makes you stop giving a damn about the rest."

Sheri set her T-shirt aside and glanced at him. His dark glasses made it tough to tell where he was looking, but she sensed he was keeping his gaze trained on her face. She knew she should probably feel self-conscious about stretch marks or her less-than-perfect muscle tone, but the sun felt so good on her skin. She closed her eyes and breathed in the ocean air and the faint scent of plumeria from the tree behind them. A whisper of breeze tickled her hair and made her nipples pucker beneath her turquoise tankini top.

"Good God."

She opened her eyes and looked at him. He shook his head and looked away, his expression chagrined behind the dark glasses. "Sorry. I didn't mean to say that out loud."

Sheri laughed as something warm and liquid spread through her limbs, and she knew it wasn't just the sunlight making her skin prickle pleasantly. She wriggled out of her shorts and folded them neatly, setting them aside. "Last week a guy whistled at me when I walked by a construction site and I was so thrilled I actually called Kelli to tell her," she said. "At this point in my life, I'm not even going to pretend to take offense at being ogled by a man."

Sam nodded, his expression stoic and his eyes still hidden behind the dark sunglasses. "In that case, I have to say you look fucking amazing." He glanced back at the twins asleep in the canopy. "Sorry guys."

She laughed again and resisted the urge to toss her hair like a supermodel. "I doubt they took offense, and neither did I."

"Seriously, you're hotter now than you were in college in that white bikini with the little strings that tied here and—"

"God, I'd forgotten that bikini. How on earth do you remember that when I can't even remember meeting you?" She shook her head as she heard her own words replay in her mind. "Sorry, I hope that's not rude."

"No ruder than me ogling you in a bikini," he said. "Then or now."

"Then we're even." Sheri picked up her book, unashamed of the bodice-ripping cover. "Thanks, Sam."

"Don't mention it."

She flopped over onto her stomach, resting her chin on her folded T-shirt. She'd only read two paragraphs when she felt the gentle stroke of his fingers in the small of her back.

She turned to look at him, holding her breath in hopes

he wouldn't stop.

"Sunscreen," he said. "And sand. You had a big gob of it stuck to you, and I didn't want you to end up burned in some weird shape."

Her skin tingled where his fingers had brushed against her, and she prayed for gobs of sunscreen decorating every inch of her flesh so he'd have a reason to touch her and touch her and touch her again.

No, she scolded herself. *Don't go there. You're a new mom with a new job and a new divorce, and the last thing you need is a distraction like this.*

No matter how delicious the distraction might be.

Chapter Six

That move at the beach had been dumb. Really dumb.

Which one? Sam's subconscious goaded him. *The part where you freaked out and tackled her over a senior citizen beachcombing with a metal detector, the part where you ogled her nipples perking up under her bikini top, or the part where you invented gobs of sunscreen just for the excuse to touch her?*

God, he was never going to make it at this rate.

He kept his distance after they returned home from the beach, grilling steaks on the barbecue and making some sort of carrot dish he found in a cookbook. It ended up tasting funny after he burned the butter, and he'd had to Google what the hell "julienne" meant before throwing in the towel and just slicing the damn things, along with his finger.

Sheri hadn't noticed any of it, thank God. Nor had she seemed to mind when Sam made himself a plate and took it to his room with an excuse about needing to spend time calling family back home. The urge to touch her, to take her in his arms and kiss her senseless, was so intense he felt dizzy.

By Sunday morning, he was going stir-crazy. He needed to get out of the house and clear his head before he did something dumb or dangerous. Or both.

When Sheri informed him she wanted the day alone with the boys before starting her new job Monday morning, he nearly wept with relief.

It was the perfect excuse for him to take a drive and scope out Sheri's new workplace. He'd never been to the Pacific Missile Range Facility, and he knew there was usually a long waiting period filled with extensive background checks for anyone who wished to visit. You couldn't get clearance without proper documentation and proof you owned a vehicle registered on the island.

But Mac's connections and Sam's military background made the whole thing a snap, which is how Sam found himself handing over his ID and paperwork to the armed, uniformed soldier at the entry gate.

"We'll hold on to these here at the gate during your visit, sir," the soldier informed him as he set aside Sam's documents. "We'll cross-check everything on your way out, too."

He handed everything over gratefully, making note of the security systems in place. Though his own military credentials had helped, Sam knew he couldn't have gotten in this quickly without Mac pulling government strings. There was normally a lengthy waiting period for visitors at PMRF, which was a good thing when it came to Limpdick. If Sheri's ex showed up on Kauai, he'd have a tough time gaining access to the compound on short notice.

Tough, but not impossible.

It was vital to get the lay of the land, to understand potential threats when Sheri was at work during the day.

"Thank you," he said to the guard. "I appreciate your service."

"Sir," the man said, and gave him a salute. "Enjoy your day."

"Mahalo," he said, and drove forward, breathing in the warm salty air, appreciating the fact that he'd been able to find a family-friendly Jeep with tons of safety features and plenty of room for the boys' car seats. He had to hand it to Mac for having the foresight—not to mention the means—to buy a vehicle for Sam. Renting would have been complicated, and buying the Jeep gave Mac the added bonus of being able to gift it to Sheri once Sam's tour was over in two weeks.

Two weeks.

He felt a pang of sadness at the thought of things ending, which was stupid. He kept his eyes on the road, cruising past the fitness facility, past the Navy Exchange and the post office, past the car wash and racquetball court. He drove by an outdoor movie theater where he imagined holding Sheri's hand under the stars as they ate popcorn and snuggled beneath a blanket.

Focus, he commanded himself as he parked and got out of the Jeep. *You're here for business. Here to make sure Sheri is safe at all times and that her asshole ex can't get anywhere near her.*

He grabbed the fishing pole and tackle box he'd bought back in town, figuring it was a good excuse if anyone grew suspicious of his presence there. There wasn't anything in particular he was looking for. He just wanted to have the lay of the land, to know where Sheri would be spending her days and how hard or easy it might be to protect her if the need arose.

The sun was beating down on him, so he stripped off his shirt and tucked it into the back of his shorts.

"Mornin'."

He turned to see an older man in a red-and-white-striped derby hat who was following the same path toward the Kinikini ditch. The man smiled and lifted his own tackle box. "Good day for fishing."

"Looking forward to it," Sam replied.

"They've got an unscheduled flight coming in shortly. Better stick to the north of the windsock or they'll make you relocate."

Sam nodded and tipped his baseball cap. "I appreciate that."

"You new around here?"

Sam nodded. "Just on the island for a couple weeks doing a favor for an old buddy."

"Ah—good place for that. I take it you're a Marine?"

"Sir?"

"Your ink." He nodded at the tattoo on Sam's shoulder. "Looks like a devil dog, if I'm not mistaken. I was a Marine, too. You still serving?"

"I'm—uh—taking a little time off. Regrouping."

"Got it. Say no more. Well, it was good meeting you. Good luck with the fishing." He tipped his derby hat and continued on his way.

"You, too," Sam called after him, watching him disappear down the path.

He continued exploring, checking out the grounds while

pausing every now and then to cast a line or watch the Navy planes flying low against the blue sky. Eventually, he made his way back to the car and headed toward Shenanigans, the café near the south end of the compound. He ordered a sausage pizza and sat jotting notes to himself while he munched.

Investigate Jonathan Price, he wrote, taking a bite of pizza.

It made him uneasy knowing Sheri's ex was here in Hawaii. Mac's latest intelligence confirmed Limpdick was staying put in Honolulu, but it wouldn't take much for the guy to hop on a puddle-jumper and show up on her doorstep. Did Limpdick have family on Kauai? Did he have any other reason to visit the Garden Isle, or was it possible he'd just wait in Honolulu until his leave was up and he had to report to his new command? Did Limpdick know where Sheri lived?

He made a note to ask Mac for more details.

Mac had said the family worried Sheri might feel vulnerable enough to take Limpdick back. That her urge to do the right thing for her babies might make her cave to pressure from the ex to get back together. It was worth keeping an eye on things, but from what Sam had observed so far, Sheri seemed stronger than her brothers gave her credit for.

He tapped his pen on the table and forced himself to keep his mind on his task list.

Make friends with the neighbors, Sam jotted, putting a star by it for emphasis. He'd seen a neighborhood watch sign on the street where Sheri lived. Might be smart to introduce himself to a few people, maybe volunteer to help. If Limpdick came sniffing around, it would be smart to have neighbors keeping an eye out for him.

Install better locks at the house. Surely Sheri couldn't argue with that, especially if he explained he was doing it to keep the babies safe.

He jotted a few more notes to himself, including a reminder to research Price's mistress. Both Mac and Sheri had mentioned the affair, and they'd said she was a stripper in Arkansas. Was she still there? Sam wanted to find out.

Thinking about Sheri made his gut twist, and he tapped the pen on the paper, distracted. He knew it was dumb to harbor a longtime crush on a girl he'd only met once at a party in college. *Dumb*, which is why he felt okay taking the job. Crushes were harmless, and nothing that would impact his ability to do his job. Certainly nothing that would cause him to break his promise to Mac about not laying a hand on her.

You already laid a hand on her, idiot.

He frowned, remembering his roving hands on the beach. Okay, so he'd screwed up. It wouldn't happen again. He'd make sure of it.

He shook his head and picked up the pen again. A college crush was a manageable thing, but things felt different now that he was here. Now that he'd met the grownup version of Sheri and realized what a stunning, intelligent, sexy woman she'd turned out to be—he was feeling a lot more than a crush. He didn't know what to call it, but he knew he needed to be careful.

Much more cautious than he'd been the last time he'd screwed up and other people paid the ultimate price.

Sam finished off the pizza and closed his notebook. He trudged back to the car and made the return trip to Sheri's house. The breeze was warm and fragrant, and he felt grateful

the Jeep gave him the option for fresh air instead of air-conditioning. The smell of the sea and the island plumeria was a good reminder that this was a pretty sweet job.

Just be careful, he reminded himself.

When he walked through the door of her house, the smell of warm garlic and sage hit him sharply in the gut, giving him an odd pang of longing for his mother. He moved tentatively into the kitchen, surprised to see no one there. The oven was on, so he peered inside. A baking sheet sat cheerfully in the middle, covered with neat rows of chicken thighs covered in something crispy and brown.

"Potato flake chicken," a voice said behind him, and he turned to see Sheri standing in the doorway. She wore a pale-gray skirt and a sea-green top made out of some sort of silky material that wrapped around her torso and draped elegantly over her lovely, freckled shoulders.

He opened his mouth to say something intelligent, but all he got out was, "Guh."

She laughed and padded barefoot into the kitchen, nudging him aside with one hip to check something in a pot on the stovetop. "Thanks, I think. I was just trying on some of the outfits I bought when I went shopping with Kelli the other day. I was thinking about this one for my first day. Does this skirt make my butt look big?"

She stepped back from the stove and did a quick pirouette, giving a self-conscious little laugh as her bare toes squeaked on the tile floor. He opened his mouth to say something, but his tongue failed him again. "Ung."

He cleared his throat and stepped back, feeling hot all of a sudden. Must be the oven. "You look—wow. I mean yes. No. That is, uh—your butt. Great. Really. I have to go check my—something."

He backed into the counter and looked for an escape route, dimly aware that the wall wasn't the best option. He thought about punching his way through it, but decided to brave the danger and edge past her. She had bent over the oven by then, poking at the chicken with a fork and squinting against the intense heat.

He did his best not to bump her, not to come into contact with those fragrant curls or the silky blouse that hugged her curves or that perfect, shapely ass. Good God, it was hot in the kitchen.

Escape.

He made a beeline for his room, and was halfway through the dining area before he realized he hadn't properly answered her question.

"You look amazing," he yelled from that distance, not willing to go back into the danger zone for anything. "You'll knock 'em dead at work."

"Thanks," she yelled back, looking mildly perplexed as she pushed the oven door shut with her hip. "Dinner's ready in ten minutes. I felt like cooking since it's my last day at home. It's nothing gourmet like you make, and nothing super-nutritious and organic like *normal moms* whip up, but it's good comfort food if you want it."

He nodded and hustled to his manny cell, closing the door behind him. He leaned heavily against it, shaking his head over his own stupidity. Even now, his hands were twitching with the urge to touch her. He couldn't believe how close he'd come to reaching out just to feel her body, warm and lush beneath that silky top. Or to stroke the curve of her backside through the skirt.

"Comfort food," he repeated, still breathing heavily. "Not the sort of comfort I need right now," he murmured, and went to take a cold shower.

. . .

Sheri swallowed her last bite of mashed potatoes, savoring the final, buttery bite as she put down her fork. Dinner had gone pretty well, considering. The chicken had been perfectly crunchy, with just enough Parmesan and pepper mixed in with the potato flakes to make the skin crisp and flavorful. It wasn't fancy, but it was one of the few things Sheri could remember her mom cooking for their big military family.

Sam had been quiet throughout the meal, though he'd had two helpings and still managed to spoon mashed carrots into Jeffrey's mouth, while she took care of feeding Jackson. Having an extra set of hands around was incredible, though it took every ounce of strength Sheri had not to think lusty thoughts about those hands. She imagined his broad fingers roaming across her body, making her whimper and wriggle beneath his touch.

She took a shower after dinner, eager to clear her head. She'd been foolish to ask his opinion on the skirt. She'd meant it innocently enough, but what had she been thinking? Why would any man in his right mind answer the question "does this make my butt look big?" Apparently, she'd gone too long without a man in the house. She'd forgotten the basic rules of coed cohabitation.

Still, it felt good to have him ogle her. Maybe too good.

After she'd bathed the twins and Sam had scrubbed the kitchen, she tucked the boys into their cribs. She was just patting Jackson's back when Sam poked his head into the room.

"I think I'll turn in a little early," he said. "Big day tomorrow. For both of us, I guess. You've got your first day of work, and I've got my first full day alone with the little guys."

Jeffrey gurgled happily in response, and Jackson batted at the mobile dangling over their cribs. Sheri smiled.

"They already know your voice," she said. "They like you."

"I like them." He hesitated in the doorway, watching her, watching the twins. "You heard from your ex lately?"

She frowned. "Why do you ask?"

"No reason. Mac mentioned he'd been calling. Asked me to keep an eye out for him."

"I've had a few voicemails from him. Stupid stuff about getting back together. I'm sure he's just drunk dialing."

"Let me know if you hear from him again, okay?"

"Why?"

"I'd just feel better knowing if he plans to show up here and see the boys. Or you."

"I doubt it'll come to that. Jonathan's not one to follow through." She frowned, wondering if she should be annoyed by the line of questioning. He sounded nosy, maybe even a little possessive, but she couldn't seem to work up any real indignation about it. Besides, it was Sam's home, too, at least for now.

She yawned, too tired to give any more thought to the matter. "I think I'm going to head to bed."

"Sleep well."

"You, too. Thanks for everything, Sam."

"No problem. It's my job." He hesitated again. "It is a job, you know. I have to be careful about not crossing any lines or doing anything that might create an unprofessional environment or jeopardize our working relationship or—"

"I get it," she interrupted, feeling her cheeks flush. She looked down at her babies so she wouldn't have to meet his eyes. "I won't ask you any more questions about my butt."

"Good." He cleared his throat, hesitating again. "But since you already asked me that one, and since I did a pretty lousy job answering it, let me just state for the record that you have the most spectacular ass I've ever seen in my life." He swallowed, then nodded. "I needed to put that out there in case there was any confusion."

"I appreciate that," she said, stifling the urge to giggle or smile or do anything else that would give her away as a wanton hussy instead of a demure, mild-mannered mother of two. "Thank you for clarifying."

"If you could refrain from mentioning that to your brother, I'd appreciate it."

"Noted." She hid her smile behind her hand.

He nodded again. "Good night, Sheri."

And with that, he wandered off down the hall.

• • •

Sleep didn't come easily that night for Sheri.

She wanted to pretend it was the nervous jitters of starting a new job in the morning, but that was only part of it. She felt dizzy with the knowledge that Sam was sleeping just inches away through the thin walls painted apricot on his side and pale turquoise on hers.

How had that happened?

Not the wall colors, though that was odd, too. How had

she come to be a single mother of twins with a gorgeous, sensitive, sexy man sleeping in another room instead of in her bed?

Not that she needed another macho guy in her bed. Jonathan had been plenty for one lifetime, thank you very much. There were times she wondered what she'd seen in him, but mostly she knew. Security. Strength. The familiarity of a big, strong military man who reminded her of her father, her mother, her brothers, her uncles, and pretty much every other member of the Patton family for as far back as Sheri could remember.

Not that there was anything wrong with the military, per se, but Jonathan had made her aware of a pattern. He, like so many of his friends, was a macho, knuckle-dragging jerk who cared more about climbing the ranks than climbing into bed with her and telling her she was smart or beautiful or that she made him see stars when they kissed.

Sam's different, whispered a tiny voice in her head. *And he's not military.*

Maybe so, she whispered back. *But Sam is off-limits.*

Right now, with a new job and new single motherhood, she needed a nanny, not a man. She needed him to do a job, not to do *her.* He was here to help her juggle it all—the career, the babies, the house—and she couldn't risk a distraction that might cause one of them to drop the ball.

Of course, they had agreed this was a trial period. If Sam moved on in a couple weeks and she found a different nanny, maybe then she and Sam could—

Stop it!

She rolled over to adjust the baby monitor, hoping to hear the breathy little murmurs of her sons' sleep sounds.

Then she remembered Sam's insistence that she leave it with him for the night.

"It's your first day at your new job tomorrow," he'd reminded her after dinner. "My whole job is centered around making it easier for you to be a working mother. If they need to be fed or changed in the middle of the night, it makes sense for me to handle it."

She hadn't argued, and she'd appreciated his foresight. But now she longed for the comfort of their sleepy little murmurs. Maybe she should just peek in on them…

She was out of bed and wrapping herself in her purple satin robe before she'd even completed the thought. She tiptoed down the tiled hallway, careful not to make any noises that could wake Sam or the babies.

Their bedroom smelled like baby shampoo and talcum powder, and she breathed it in, feeling calmer already. She took a few steps toward the cribs and peered down. Their little bodies were pressed close to the bars, and Jeffrey had reached through to curl his fingers around his brother's big toe. Jackson slurped his fingers and made breathy little sounds in his sleep.

"You guys are the best," she whispered softly, resisting the urge to touch them. No sense waking them up.

She watched them a few more moments before stepping away from the cribs. She turned and tiptoed toward the door, pivoting one last time to gaze at their little sleeping forms in the glow of the nightlight. Then she stepped into the hallway with her eyes still on the cribs, feeling her way along the wall.

A hand clapped over her mouth and Sheri struggled to scream as she collided with a solid wall of muscle.

Chapter Seven

Sam held Sheri still as he lowered his lips to her ear.

"It's just me," he whispered. "You ran into me before I could let you know I was here, and I didn't want you to scream and wake the boys."

She sagged against him, and he resisted the urge to savor the lush, slippery heat of her body pressed against his. He released her, and she stepped around him, moving out of the boys' room and into the hall.

"Oh," she gasped, reaching for the tie on her robe. Somehow it had come undone in the collision, and it took every ounce of strength he had not to steal a glimpse at what was underneath.

Fuck it. He wasn't that strong. He looked down and saw an endless expanse of creamy skin. No nightie. No T-shirt. No sleep shorts. Just Sheri.

His heart throbbed hard. Among other things.

"Now I know," he murmured.

"Know what?" she asked, cinching the waist belt on the robe and peering up at him in the darkness.

"Know what you sleep in." He swallowed.

She let go of her robe and studied him, close enough that her breath grazed his chest. "That's something you were wondering?"

He nodded, too dizzy to speak.

"You were in your bed thinking about me?" she whispered. There was something conflicted in her eyes, something uncertain.

But there was something heated there, too.

He gritted his teeth, knowing he should step back but unable to make his feet move. A small ghost of a smile crossed her face in the dim light, so faint he might've missed it.

But he didn't miss the note of desire in her voice when she spoke again. "Dammit, I want you."

Then she lunged for him.

He might've staggered if he hadn't been braced for her. Instead, he moved back against the wall, letting the warm, smooth weight of her body press him back against the doorframe.

He hadn't bothered with a shirt when he'd gotten up to check the boys, and he thanked the heavens for that now. He could feel every inch of her warm, lush flesh pressed against the front of the silky robe, the only thing separating him from all that beautiful nakedness.

"Kiss me," she gasped, not waiting for a response. She arched up on tiptoes and found his lips with hers, kissing him with a dizzying heat that made Sam groan low in his throat.

He responded by sliding his hands over her hips and

up, savoring the heat of her body beneath the smooth satin. His fingers traced every curve, trying to memorize her as he kissed her softly at first, then harder.

Sheri wriggled against him, her breasts pressing firmly into his chest. He could feel her nipples through the satin, and the minty taste of her mouth made him dizzy with need. His hands had continued their journey up her torso, and he found himself gripping her rib cage, feathering his thumbs over the undersides of her breasts.

"I shouldn't do this," she murmured, then did it again, kissing him harder as she pressed her body against his.

"God," he whispered back, slipping one hand down to find the tie she'd just fastened. He gave it a tug and felt the material slip back, baring her shoulders. Sam reached up to brush the fabric back and broke their kiss to trail his lips over that warm, freckled curve. He kissed his way across the plane of her shoulders, dipping low above her collarbones until he came to the soft, fragrant hollow under her ear.

He was light-headed now, all the blood in his body having surged to his groin the instant she'd whispered, *I want you.*

Sam groaned as her fingers danced over the front of his boxers. He could feel her grazing, stroking, squeezing until he thought he'd lose his mind.

He fought to remember why he wasn't supposed to do this, fought harder to keep himself under control.

He wasn't winning in either case. He moaned again and kissed her hard on that warm, soft mouth. Her breasts were full and tight pressed against his chest, and he swore he'd never felt anything so mind-blowingly soft in his life.

"You're killing me," he hissed through clenched teeth.

"We shouldn't—"

A plaintive cry from the next room stopped him from articulating whatever it was they shouldn't do.

Not that it wasn't clear to both of them.

She took a step back, blinking in the dim glow of the hallway night-light as she reached down to retie her robe. "I'm so sorry. I don't know what came over me—"

"Not your fault," he said. "I'll handle the boys. Please. Go back to bed. You need your sleep."

The look in her eyes told him that wasn't all she needed. He felt the same way, but Mac's words echoed in his head.

Keep your hands off my sister.

"Good night," Sam whispered, and stepped away from her into the darkness of the tiny bedroom.

· · ·

On her lunch break the next day, Sheri scurried out to a private spot on the beach near her office and dialed Kelli from her cell phone.

"I was hoping I'd hear from you!" Kelli yelled cheerfully over the cacophony of barking at her vet clinic. "How's the first day at the new job?"

"Good. I just called home and Sam says the boys are doing well."

"That's a relief."

She toed off her shoes and settled on a log, careful not to wrinkle her new skirt as she buried her toes in warm sand. "Look, there's something I want to ask you."

"Fire away. The bulldog who swallowed a sock isn't due for another fifteen minutes."

She bit her lip, not sure where to start. "That seminar you took a few years ago—the one about sexual harassment in the workplace?"

There was a long pause, followed by an exasperated groan. "Seriously? You're being harassed on your first day of work?"

"No! Of course not. I was just wondering about the laws concerning sexual relationships between employers and employees and whether—"

"Oh my God, you slept with Sam!"

Sheri cringed and pulled the phone away from her face, then worried Kelli's shouts might carry all the way to Hanalei even without the phone. She put the phone back to her ear and lowered her own voice.

"I didn't sleep with Sam," she insisted, surprised to find the corners of her mouth turning up in a smile. There was something deliciously naughty about saying the words aloud. "But I would have."

"What on earth stopped you? Jesus, I had to restrain myself from jumping him on your front porch when he said hello."

She rolled her eyes. "There are these two small people living in my house. Maybe you've met them? They tend to cry at the drop of a hat and wake up at the most inconvenient times—"

"Got it. Say no more. So the babies interrupted you before you could bump uglies with the manny, and now you're wondering if you could be arrested?"

"Pretty much." She picked up a piece of driftwood and began poking holes in the sand, wondering about the prospect of spending time behind bars for a few innocent kisses.

They weren't that innocent.

Kelli laughed. "Unless you handcuffed him to the bed and groped him against his will, I think you're okay."

Sheri's brain veered a little at that, and she caught herself picturing his massive hands shackled to either side of her headboard, his broad chest glistening with baby oil as she lowered herself onto his—

"No!" she said. "I didn't handcuff him. But still, I'm his employer, and he's my subordinate and I've been reading the PMRF staff handbook and it has all kinds of scary language about workplace relationships and sexual harassment and how to handle inappropriate fraternization. It has me worried."

Kelli was quiet a moment, and Sheri pictured her at the vet clinic neutering a rottweiler with one hand while she gripped her phone with the other. Her friend was efficient like that.

"Didn't your brother hire him?" Kelli asked.

"What?"

"Mac. I thought he hired Sam. And he said the other night that he's the one paying him, not you. Doesn't that make him your brother's employee?"

"I guess."

"So there's no problem then. As long as Sam doesn't nail your brother."

"I don't think there's much risk of that."

"Good. Because I've got dibs on Mac."

She laughed and poked her stick into the sand again. "I suppose sexual harassment is the least of my concerns. God, I can't believe I lunged at him like that. Can you think of anything dumber?"

"*Not* lunging at him?"

Sheri sighed. "Seriously, it's a bad idea. I just moved here to take this job, and I've finally gotten my life together. The last thing I need is to screw everything up by — "

"Screwing the help?"

"Exactly." She flipped the sand around with her stick, annoyed with herself for wanting him so badly. "God, I feel dumb."

"Don't. Abs like that would bring any woman to her knees. A convenient place to be, actually."

"I can't. I definitely can't. I'm not going to sleep with my manny." She winced at her own words, glancing around to make sure no one heard. There was a family about three hundred yards down the beach to the left, and some old guy with a fishing pole and a red-and-white-striped hat standing in the parking lot stuffing his tackle box into his truck. He looked up and gave her a friendly wave, and Sheri waved back, hoping her voice hadn't traveled that far.

"No sex with the manny," she insisted, ordering herself to comply. "End of story."

"I don't like stories with unhappy endings."

"Neither do I, but I've already had one unhappy ending with Jonathan. I can't risk another one."

"Seems a shame to let that prime piece of man meat go to waste, but I get it." There was some shuffling on the other end of the line, and a loud yowl that was either an angry tomcat or Kelli's latest conquest. "I've gotta go. Call if you need anything. Or if Sam takes his shirt off around the house. I can be there in five minutes."

"Thanks, Kel. Love you."

She hung up the phone and plunged her stick deep into the sand, swirling it around a few more times for good measure.

"No sex with the manny," she repeated, forcing herself to hear the words. "No matter what."

Chapter Eight

Sam bent low over the double stroller and adjusted the small hat shielding Jeffrey's face. He did the same for Jackson, stretching down to pick up the bottle of juice the little guy had dropped.

Or thrown, more likely.

"Buddy, knock it off," he murmured, retrieving the bottle from beneath a stroller the size of a small automobile. "Your mama made this for you. It has five kinds of fruit juice plus a bunch of vitamin powder and nutritious crap. She wants you to grow up big and strong and smart."

Jackson seemed to consider that for a moment, then tossed the bottle on the ground again.

Sam bent down again. "At least you're consistent."

The baby shrieked with frustration, and his brother joined in, a chorus of unhappy baby. Sam rocked the stroller again, hopeful they weren't headed for another meltdown. They'd had a rough morning after Sheri left for work, with the twins screaming for an hour straight. He'd brought them here to Smith's Tropical Paradise, hoping a stroll around the thirty-acre botanical garden on the Wailua River might offer a welcome distraction. If nothing else, the boys' shrieks blended harmoniously with the squawking of tropical birds and the constant cluck of chickens that seemed to be everywhere on this island.

"Look, buddy—it's a flower," he said for the hundredth time, pointing out something orange and shaped vaguely like a hand grenade.

The boys stopped screaming, momentarily distracted by the peacock strutting past. He couldn't blame them for being fussy, really. They probably missed their mom.

Sam could relate.

All day, he'd been catching himself mid-grin at the memory of Sheri pressing her body against his, arching her back to kiss him, demanding "Kiss me" in her breathy, delicate whisper that made his gut clench. If only they hadn't been interrupted—

"No," he said out loud, and both babies looked up. He forced another smile and patted Jeffrey's head. "Not you guys. You're doing great. Your uncle, on the other hand—"

He trailed off there, figuring it was best not to alert the boys that Uncle Mac would gleefully castrate their caregiver for what had nearly transpired outside their bedroom the night before.

He pictured her again, warm and willing and so soft pressed against him with her curls brushing her shoulder blades and twining around his fingers. God, she'd even smelled good. Like spices in the kitchen and some sort of tropical flower. And the way she'd responded when he touched her, curving her body against him, nipping little kisses down his throat, driving him mad with heat and desire and those sweet little moans.

"Your mom," he murmured to the boys with a reverence that surprised him. He bent down to retrieve the bottle again, tucking it into the back pocket of the stroller before handing the baby a teething ring instead. "She is some kind of woman."

Jeffrey yawned, while Jackson gummed the teething ring a few times, then tossed it out of the stroller. Sam caught it with one hand before a peacock could peck it. He tugged off the stretchy band holding his sunglasses around his neck and coiled it around the ring. Tying a couple knots, he secured it to the top of the stroller. Then he tested it out, making sure there was no way the little guy could strangle himself.

"There you go. Try throwing it now." He handed the ring back to Jeffrey, who frowned, then put it in his mouth.

Sam straightened up and pushed the stroller forward, pushing aside his thoughts of Sheri at the same time.

Keep your hands off my sister.

Mac's words echoed in his ears, and he shook his head to clear his remaining visions of Sheri. Aside from Mac's order, there were a million reasons getting involved with her was a terrible idea. The ink was barely dry on her divorce papers, and the last thing she needed was another messy relationship. Especially not with a military jerk.

She doesn't know you're military, his subconscious pointed out, and he felt a stab of guilt for lying to her.

Her declaration about lying and Mac's warning about touching Sheri bounced around Sam's brain in a cacophony of angry words. It would be stupid to get involved. He was here to protect her, to keep her idiot ex away from her and the boys. Mac had made the mission pretty clear.

And the last thing he needed was to screw up another job by failing to follow orders.

"It won't happen again, I swear," he said aloud, more for his own sake than for the babies. They gurgled in the stroller, and Jackson waved one fat little fist as if in salute to the giant rooster strutting past. A peacock fanned his tail nearby, turning in circles to show his vibrant plumage to a female. The air was heavy with the smell of tropical flowers and the buzz of insects. It certainly was beautiful here.

He looked fondly down at the boys. Jeffrey squealed and tried to throw the teething ring again, then shrieked as it spun overhead like a piñata.

"I've got this situation under control," he added, giving the babies a reassuring smile.

Jackson smiled back and farted. At least, Sam thought that's all it was. Then he saw the telltale seepage leaking through the onesie and realized he'd made a terrible miscalculation.

"Oh, shit."

Literally.

Jackson started laughing, but it quickly turned to howls of distress. Jeffrey joined in, wailing with an urgency that made the peacocks scatter.

Frantic, Sam patted himself down, looking for something to make the noise stop. "I forgot the diaper bag. Dammit." He scanned the gardens, hoping to see some other parent strolling nearby with the necessary provisions.

There was no one.

Sam was on his own in this bizarre, foreign jungle with

two comrades equally unprepared for this mission. He scooped up the baby, glancing around for a faucet or some-place he could clean the little guy.

Jackson howled louder.

"Don't worry," he panted. "I've got your back, buddy. Semper fi."

Cradling the baby in one arm, Sam jerked his dive knife out of the pocket on the back of the stroller. He'd felt silly stashing it there when he left the house, but now he was grateful to have this crucial tool of his trade.

"Hang on, man—I'll get you out of this."

Sam slid the blade between the buttonholes on the onesie. With one swift stroke, he sliced the stained fabric from the baby's delicate skin. Jackson blinked, mesmerized into silence. Sam made quick work of the diaper, letting it drop to the ground like a fallen warrior.

A really smelly fallen warrior.

"I've got you," Sam told Jackson, striding toward the pond ten feet away. He called over his shoulder to his brother in arms. "You stay put, Jeffrey! I'm not leaving, I swear. I've never left a man behind."

"Behind," Sam repeated, turning his attention back to the naked behind entrusted to his care. "Sorry, man—it's the only way."

He stooped down and stuck a finger in the water to test the temperature. Finding it pleasant, he took a deep breath and plunged Jackson's bare bottom into the pond. The baby squealed, equal parts confusion and delight. Sam swished him around making motorboat noises as he washed away evidence of a hard-fought battle.

Sam lurched upright again, spinning the baby around in

an effort to air dry him. Jackson waved his arms, enthralled with his own nakedness.

"I know the feeling," he muttered, sprinting back to the stroller to search for anything resembling a diaper. Could he weave one from palm fronds? Fashion something out of peacock feathers?

Nope. There was only one option.

"Sometimes a man has to make sacrifices on the battlefield," Sam said solemnly, placing Jackson back in the stroller.

Straightening, Sam picked up his dive knife and grabbed the hem of his favorite Tennessee Titans T-shirt. He sliced it from his body, stretching the fabric out to form a crude sling.

Grabbing Jackson again, Sam dropped to his knees with the T-shirt spread on the grass in front of him. He placed Jackson on it, swaddling the baby awkwardly with the soft fabric. He looped shreds of navy cotton to create a sort of loincloth, careful to make sure all the vital parts were covered. He folded and tied, fashioning a bowline on a bight, a half hitch, and several more knots he'd forgotten the names for.

When he finished, Sam sat back on his heels and wiped his brow, admiring his work. It didn't look half-bad. From a distance, it almost resembled a onesie with a built-in diaper.

"There," he said, patting Jackson's belly. "It's not pretty, but it'll do the job."

Jackson smacked his heels on the grass and laughed, a musical baby giggle that made Sam smile in spite of himself. In the stroller, Jeffrey hooted with glee. Sam stood up and tickled Jeffrey's belly as he put Jackson back in the stroller.

"Don't you go crapping yourself, too," Sam told Jeffrey

as he strapped the other twin in beside him. "I'm fresh out of T-shirts."

He tickled each baby again, making them both giggle harder. Another peacock strutted by, intrigued by the noises, and the babies squealed. Sam reached into his pocket and pulled out the Baggie of birdseed. He tossed out a handful, and the boys chorused with joyful shrieks as peacocks ran from all directions to claim their prize.

Sam was so focused on the task that he didn't hear the sound of approaching footsteps.

"Sam?"

He whirled around to see Sheri standing beside him, a strange expression on her face. She looked lovely and sun-kissed and very, very perplexed.

"Sheri—what are you doing here?"

"I saw your note on the kitchen table," she said, stepping closer with her eyes flicking across his chest. "I got off a little early since I was just doing orientation stuff. I hadn't been out here to explore the gardens yet, so I thought I'd come join you and check the place out. Um, Sam?"

"Yeah?"

"I know Kauai's a casual island, but they usually want people to wear shirts in a place like this."

"Right. Um, yeah. Got it. Just wanted to get a little sun while we're strolling the gardens." He kept his back turned away from her, making sure she didn't spot the tattoo on his shoulder blade.

She stared at him with an expression he couldn't read. Eyeing his abs or questioning his sanity? He couldn't tell. He gave her a hopeful smile, doing his best to radiate the energy of a competent, experienced caretaker.

She flushed and looked away, turning to fuss over the babies.

"How are my little guys? How are my babies? How are my best, best men?" She paused, hesitating a moment before scooping up one of the twins. "Sam?"

"Yes?"

"Why is Jackson wearing an outfit that says *tits*?"

"Tits?"

"Yes, tits. I mean, I know he's a fan and all, but—"

"Titans," Sam said, doing a mental head-smack as he looked down to see the awkwardly folded wording on his shirt. "Tennessee Titans. Yes, see, I can explain."

She gave him an expectant look, not angry or judgmental, but clearly a bit baffled.

"Right, uh, in some European cultures, there are special swaddling techniques caretakers use to create a sense of security and calm for babies experiencing traumatic events like teething or weaning or the first time being away from their mothers—"

"Swaddling techniques?"

He nodded, knowing he was digging himself in deeper here, but not seeing any way out. "How about I tell you all about it over dinner?" he said, nodding toward the exit. "And you can tell me all about your first day at work. Did things go well?"

"Very well," she said, bending down to place Jackson back in his seat. She cooed at Jeffrey, who cooed back and reached up to touch her hair and bat at her necklace.

The interaction gave Sam a prolonged moment to take in the beautiful curve of her ass in that skirt, and he wondered what it would be like to cup his hands around it.

Or maybe if she stayed bent down like that, he could push her skirt up and slide his hands over her breasts as he moved behind her and—

"Don't you think so?"

He snapped his eyes off her ass and blinked. "I'm sorry, what did you ask?"

"It's beautiful here. I had a friend who got married at Smith Gardens. I got to stroll around for thirty minutes or so before I found you, but I'd love to come back sometime."

"The boys really seemed to enjoy it," he said. "They've been entranced by the peacocks all afternoon. I even bought some little bags of birdseed so we could feed them. The birds, not the babies. The twins didn't eat birdseed."

Much, he amended silently, thinking it best not to mention his ill-advised attempt to let the boys feed the birds. It had resulted in a quick call to Poison Control to make sure it was okay for babies to ingest small amounts of millet.

Sheri smiled. "I've always wanted to come to one of the luaus they hold here at night. I've heard they give the most amazing lays."

"Lays?" Sam's brain short-circuited, trying not to picture Sheri topless in a hula skirt.

"*Leis*. You know, rings of flowers?"

"Right. Yes, definitely. Maybe we can all come back sometime for a luau and bring the boys."

His heart twisted a little at the thought of that, knowing this happy little family charade would be over the instant Lieutenant Limpdick took off in two weeks. After that, Sheri would need a real nanny, not a bodyguard.

He looked down at the boys and smiled, making a mental note to find a pair of plush peacocks for them to remember him by.

She smiled back and began to push the stroller toward the exit while Sam made a hasty effort to scoop up the soiled onesie and diaper and stuff them into a nearby trash can. Sheri moved ahead, her hips swaying softly in her tight skirt.

"Oh, wow," she called. "I never would have thought of that."

"Of what?" he asked, wiping his hands on his shorts as he hustled to catch up with her.

"The sunglasses cord on the teething ring. You made this?"

Sam shrugged. "It solved the problem."

"You even figured out how to rig it up so he can't choke himself on the cord. You're a smarter mom than I am."

She said it with a smile, but there was something sad in her eyes. She steered the stroller over some grass and onto a paved pathway, her expression oddly wistful.

"I don't think I'd go that far," he said, following her toward the exit. "I spent ten minutes this morning trying to wipe poop off Jeffrey, only to realize I was scrubbing a birthmark."

She laughed. "It's how I tell them apart sometimes. Is that bad to admit? That I can't tell my own children apart? God, I'm sure *normal moms*—"

"Why do you always say that?"

She gave him a startled look. "What?"

"That crap about normal moms. What the hell is a *normal* mom?"

She studied him for a moment, then looked away, maneuvering the stroller over a bump in the paved path. "It always seems like all the other moms out there were implanted with some sort of mommy chip. Something that gives them instant skills at properly dressing their babies and soothing owies and singing lullabies and all of that. I'm just standing here hoping no one notices I put my kid's diaper on backward."

Sam shook his head. "You look like you've got it pretty dialed in to me."

She looked up from the pathway and gave him a small smile. "I appreciate that. But from where I stand, you've got more of a mommy chip than I do."

He felt a little twist of guilt knowing he'd handed the boys a snack of whole carrots this morning before remembering they didn't have teeth. Then he'd stood there like an idiot while Jackson tried to stick the carrot in his ear.

Mommy chip indeed.

Sam cleared his throat. "Well, if there are normal moms and abnormal moms, and you're the latter, I'll take abnormal any day of the week."

She blinked, and for a moment, he thought she might cry. "That is the nicest thing anyone's said to me all week."

He grinned, shoving his hands in his pockets to resist the urge to tuck a long curl behind her ear, or tell her he could think of a dozen nice things to say or do to her that might make her week.

"Come on, let's get home for dinner," Sam said, hoping like hell he'd be able to assemble something vaguely edible after spending an hour on the phone that morning while his sister coached him on cooking techniques. "I'm making something extra special to celebrate your first day."

"You really are amazing," she said, smiling as she pushed the stroller through the gate and out into the parking lot. "I can't believe my brother found you."

He fell into step beside her, trying not to feel like the biggest jerk on earth.

Chapter Nine

There were moments Sheri wasn't sure whether she wanted to fuck Sam or *be* Sam.

That wasn't entirely true. She pretty much always wanted to fuck him, which made for a lot of distracted meals and infant bath-times. But she also envied the hell out of him for his natural ease with everything from babies to briskets.

Okay, so the *tits* shirt had been a little weird, but maybe things were different in foreign countries where Sam had worked. She was hardly one to judge.

She sighed. The whole arrangement seemed so odd sometimes. Here she was on one end of the house changing out of her work clothes in the master bedroom, while Sam played with the boys in their bouncy seats and put the finishing touches on dinner. God, whatever it was smelled delicious. Something smoky, like ribs or barbecue or maybe kalua pork. The last time she'd tried to whip up something like that, she'd—

Hell. She'd never tried to whip up something like that. She frowned and peeled off her blouse, draping it over the back of the flowered chair beside her bed. She glanced down at her cell phone, annoyed to see Jonathan had called again. He'd left two messages this morning, both demanding to sit down and talk face-to-face about reconciliation.

She'd promptly deleted them.

"Hey, Sheri?" Sam yelled from the kitchen. Sheri froze, topless and exposed and—well, yeah, a little excited at the prospect of having any sort of connection with Sam when she wasn't fully dressed. She considered not responding, just for the thrill of hearing him shout her name again.

"Yes?" she called back, toeing off her kitten-heeled sandals with the dainty straps that had been cutting into her feet all day.

"Take your time getting dressed, okay?" he called. "Like if you want to take a bath or something. Or even a short nap. Or how about I bring you a glass of wine to enjoy while I finish dinner?"

She rolled her eyes, wondering if he wasn't taking this domestic thing a little too seriously. Maybe she should talk with him about that, she mused as she unzipped her skirt. Or maybe Mac had ordered him to wait on her hand and foot. A girl could get used to that. After so many years with a man whose idea of foreplay was asking her to hold his feet while he did ab crunches, having a generous, competent, domestically inclined man around the house was an incredible treat.

She slipped off her skirt and folded it, draping it over the chair with her blouse. She knew she should hang them both up or set them aside for dry cleaning, but her closet space was abysmal and she didn't have the energy to hunt down hangers and figure out the proper place for everything. That was something she'd need to address soon, along with all the other maintenance issues on the house.

She turned and caught sight of herself in the full-length mirror and quickly sucked in her stomach. She didn't look too bad for a woman who'd given birth seven months ago, but this sure as hell wasn't the body she used to have. Would Sam mind? What if she'd tried to seduce him last night and he laughed or said he wasn't interested or—

"Sheri?" he called again, his voice sounding closer than the kitchen this time. "Just stay put and I'll bring the wine to you, okay?"

Crap, had she remembered to lock the door? She grabbed her robe off the hook by the dresser and tugged it on, her arm tangling in the purple satin. She cinched the belt around her waist and cracked open the door.

Sam stood in the hallway with a sheepish look and a glass of white wine gripped in his big hand. "Here you go. Chardonnay. From the Willamette Valley in Oregon."

She opened the door a little wider, but didn't reach for the glass. "Thank you, Sam, but I can come out to the kitchen myself and—"

"No! I mean, just hang out in here." He thrust the glass at her, and she had no choice but to take it.

"Thank you," she said, shivering a little at the sight of his powerful, well-muscled form blocking her doorway. "The boys are still doing okay?"

"They're great! Everything's under control. Just take your time and enjoy the wine. Relax a little in your room."

"Sure, fine," she said, taking a sip of wine to show him she was paying attention.

"Dinner's—um, not quite ready. I'll come get you when it is, okay?"

"Okay, okay. You're the boss." She felt her cheeks redden. "I mean my brother's the boss. Not me. I'm not technically your employer, in case there was any question of—"

"Your brother. Got it." He nodded once, and she took a big gulp of wine. "I'll come get you when dinner's ready," he said again.

"Okay. Thank you for the wine."

"You're welcome," he said, and gave her something that looked like an aborted salute.

She waved back and closed the door, setting the wine on top of the dresser.

Well, that was weird.

She glanced back at the door, wondering what he would have done if she'd grabbed the front of his T-shirt and pulled him into the room. It was a small room, just a few steps to the bed where she could push him back onto the flowered coverlet and—

Sheri frowned at her bed. "Hey, Sam?" she yelled, wondering if he could hear her if he was back in the kitchen again.

"Yeah?" he called back, the bang of the oven door punctuating his sentence.

"Did you make my bed?"

There was a short silence. "Yeah. Did I do it wrong?"

She trailed a finger over her quilt, pretty sure she hadn't seen such a tightly made bed since the morning her father donned his general's uniform, rounded up the Patton children, and barked a lesson on the proper way to make a bed to military standards. Hospital corners at precise forty-five-degree angles, sheets so crisp they looked like they'd been ironed, the flowers on the coverlet perfectly aligned with the ones on the pillowcases.

Christ, how long had that taken him?

"You could seriously bounce a quarter off this bed," she yelled. "Thank you."

"You're welcome."

She pressed her palm into the mattress, thinking a quarter wasn't what she most wanted to bounce there. The thought of Sam's big hands smoothing her sheets and squeezing her pillows into submission made her shiver. She loosened the tie on her robe and slid a hand inside, absently stroking her palm up the curve of her rib cage. Her hands were half the size of his, but she trailed her fingers across her breast anyway. She cupped it softly at first, then with a firmer touch.

God, what would it be like to have his hand there instead, stroking the heated flesh, testing the weight of it in his big, work-roughened hands? She circled one finger around her nipple, gasping as a slow flicker of pleasure swelled up from her belly. She shrugged off the robe, letting it fall in a warm, satin puddle at her feet.

She kicked the robe aside, standing there in her bra and panties under the soft flutter of her ceiling fan. Her bedroom window was open just a little, and Sheri breathed in the scent of ocean air and fresh-cut grass as she drew another finger over her breast, thrilled at the way her nipple tightened in response.

She glanced over her shoulder, wondering if she should lock the door. What if he came back and discovered her touching herself like this?

Good, she thought. *Let him watch.*

Let him help.

That was crazy thinking, and she knew she didn't mean it. She couldn't *really* have him. But maybe she could pretend.

Her heart was thudding hard now, and she pressed her whole palm over her nipple, squeezing and circling and making herself dizzy with pleasure.

Smiling to herself, she imagined Sam's hands roaming over her like this, claiming her. She leaned back against the dresser and caught the wineglass with her free hand, lifting it to her lips. The liquid was cool with a citrusy tang, and she let it slide down her throat as she imagined Sam's hands traveling her heated flesh, exploring every curve. She set the glass back down and moved her palm over her abdomen, making a few lazy circles there before slipping beneath the waistband of her panties.

It wasn't hard to picture Sam touching her like that, pushing the warm satin down over her hips. She peeled off her panties and toed them aside, her breath coming faster as one finger slid lower, grazing her most sensitive spot once, twice. She let her fingertip linger right there.

Gasping, she began making slow, delicate circles as she leaned back against the hard wood of the dresser. Her elbow bumped the wineglass, but it didn't spill. She wasn't sure she'd care if it did, as she moved her legs apart and used her finger to spread herself open.

Her breath caught again as the cool whisper of the ceiling fan fluttered over her flesh, between her legs. She dipped her finger inside herself, imagining Sam's hand pressing against her, testing her wetness.

God, she wanted him.

Her nipples were tight and achy against the thin cups of her bra, and Sheri leaned hard on the dresser, letting it hold her weight. She pictured Sam moving down between her legs, his stubbled cheek brushing the inside of her thighs as he dropped to his knees on the carpet, parting her legs with his chin. His breath was warm on her flesh, his tongue probing softly between—

"Sheri?"

She froze. His voice was distant, probably still in the kitchen, but her pulse kicked up anyway.

"Yes?" she called back, her voice high and tight. She should probably lock the door, but she didn't want to move her hand and—

"Where's the fire extinguisher?" he called.

"Fire extinguisher?" She blinked, trying to make sense of the words.

"I'm just doing a safety check," he called. "Wanted to make sure you have the necessary equipment required by building regulations and fire laws and the covenants, codes, and restrictions of the neighborhood association."

Safety first, she thought, and reached over with her free hand to flip the door lock. "It's under the kitchen sink," she called. "I think."

There was another pause, followed by something crashing.

"Got it," he called. "Just relax, enjoy your wine, all right? I'll come get you when dinner's ready. It might be a few more minutes. Just stay there, okay?"

A few more minutes. Okay. She could make the most of those minutes.

She moved her fingers, dipping in and out, then circling again to bring herself back to that frenzied pitch. She closed her eyes, imagining Sam's hands on her again, his fingers clutching her thighs. She arched against him, twining her fingers in his hair as she drew him closer, urging him on.

"Yes!" she gasped. "*Sam.*"

"Yeah?" he yelled from the end of the house.

Shit.

"Nothing!" she trilled, panting harder now, praying like hell he didn't come down here.

Come. Down. Here. Right here.

Oh, God!

Everything exploded behind her eyes as wave after wave of pleasure crashed into her, knocking her back against the dresser. She gasped and writhed, bumping the wineglass with her elbow again as she plunged her finger deeper, feeling his tongue moving into her, his hands on her thighs, his breath hot on her damp flesh.

When her pulse finally slowed and the electric jolts subsided, she held her breath and listened. Had she gasped those last words aloud?

I can tell him I was watching YouTube videos before dinner, she thought.

She peeled herself off the dresser and stood shakily in the center of the room, getting her bearings. She dressed quickly, pulling on a soft yellow T-shirt and a turquoise cotton skirt. She spotted her panties on the floor, but ignored them, stepping around her robe as she moved to the bathroom.

She splashed cool water over her face, feeling flushed and decadent and a little bit naughty. Washing her hands with gardenia soap, she studied her reflection in the mirror. She didn't look too disheveled. Maybe a little flushed, and her hair was a mess of tangled curls. She ran her fingers through it, not bothering with a comb. Her cheeks were pink and glowy, and her eyes had a definite sparkle. She rubbed her lips together, then brushed on a hint of pink gloss as an afterthought.

She stepped out of the bathroom, not bothering with shoes. Unlocking the bedroom door, she hesitated, shivering at the feeling of cool air between her legs.

Maybe she should go back for her panties.

"To hell with it," she said, and stepped into the hall. Kelli had ordered her to get her mojo back. Maybe going pantyless to dinner after the best orgasm she'd had in a long time was the first step.

She reached back and grabbed the wine off the dresser, taking a small sip before padding down the tiled hall toward the front of the house. She rounded the corner, breathing in the fragrance of smoky meat. Sam must be barbecuing, or maybe he really was making kalua pork. Of course, where would he find time to dig a pit in the backyard and roast a whole pig? The idea was absurd, but then this was Sam. Those arms looked like he dug trenches in his sleep.

She passed through the dining room, the smell of smoke stronger there. She sneezed once, shielding her wine with her forearm. Where the hell was Sam?

She turned the corner to the kitchen, then froze.

"Sam?"

He stood at the rear door, his back to her as he murmured to someone outside. He whirled at the sound of her voice, a guilty expression on his face and two large white bags in his hand.

"Sheri." His Adam's apple bobbed as he swallowed. "I thought you were taking a bath. I—um—"

"That'll be thirty-two-fifty, mister," a voice said from the back porch. "Plus tip."

"Right, right," Sam said, setting the bags on the counter as he pulled his wallet out of his back pocket. He counted out a few bills, then turned back to the door and handed them to someone outside. "Keep the change."

He turned back to Sheri, looking sheepish. "There's been a slight alteration in our dinner plans."

"Cooking mishap?" She laughed and peered in one of the bags. "Oh, God. Did you order kalua pork and cabbage from that place down the street? That's my favorite."

She pulled out one of the Styrofoam boxes and looked up to see Sam's features flooded with a mix of relief and embarrassment. And maybe a little something else. His eyes flicked to her backside, and she remembered the panties on her bedroom floor. Could he tell she was going commando?

"I, um—yeah," he said, clearing his throat. "I'm used to commercial ovens, and the last place I worked had a convection oven, so the timing is a little off and the temperature must've been—"

"Don't worry about it," Sheri said, waving a hand as she pulled the rest of the boxes out of the bags. "I burn stuff all the time. I like to pretend it's a culinary technique, but obviously it isn't. There's a reason you probably saw more than one fire extinguisher under the sink."

"I wondered about that. Still, I'm really sorry. I took the burned roast out to the Dumpster already, and I opened all the windows, but—"

"Seriously, Sam. Don't worry about it." She popped the top on one of the takeout containers, plucking out a piece of pork with her fingers. She sighed with pleasure as she slipped it into her mouth. "God, that's good."

She chewed blissfully, then licked the tips of her fingers. When she looked back at Sam, he was watching her mouth with a funny expression.

She swallowed, feeling oddly guilty. "Whoops. Guess I should wait for dinnertime? And maybe for silverware."

He swallowed and reached into the cupboard for plates. "Silverware's overrated. I'm always up for using my fingers."

She flushed, resisting the urge to look at his fingers and remember where she'd envisioned them five minutes ago. She turned to rinse her hands at the sink, then dried them on a flowery dish towel. "Seriously, if I had a quarter for every time I'd burned dinner, I'd have enough to buy kalua pork every night of the week for a year."

He grinned, looking a little less sheepish now. "I thought about ditching the takeout containers and trying to pass this off as my own," he confessed. "Let me at least make a salad. I'm pretty sure I can do that without burning anything."

"I can chop veggies," she offered. "Or set the table. Or—"

"No, just sit. Drink your wine, tell me about your first day at the new job."

She hesitated, wanting to be useful. But hell, her knees still felt weak, and it was so nice to just sit down and relax, savoring the heady smell of pork and the sight of a muscular man moving around her kitchen.

She dropped into a dining room chair and picked up her wineglass, taking another sip. "There's not much to tell," she said. "It was mostly orientation stuff. A lot of rules about dress codes and holidays and sexual harassment policies and stuff."

"That'll be handy the next time you show up naked at

the office on Easter and decide to sexually harass someone."

He grabbed a knife off the counter. It was a huge knife—much bigger than Sheri would have chosen—and he handled it with a lot more force than she expected. She studied his fingers, huge and deft around the thick shaft.

She lifted her wineglass again, hoping to hide her flaming cheeks. "Right," she said into the glass, remembering her conversation with Kelli earlier that afternoon. "No sexual harassment here. No siree."

Christ, she really needed to Google the laws on employee/supervisor relations. She shouldn't be thinking this much about sleeping with a guy who lived here as her employee.

Besides, she'd just extricated herself from one bad relationship. Did she really need to risk another one?

She drained the last of her wine and set it down, watching him chop with rough, powerful strokes. It seemed like an odd approach for lettuce, not that she was any sort of expert in the kitchen. He was the one with culinary training, after all. She didn't recognize the knife, so apparently he traveled with his own kitchen tools.

"You wield that knife like you're trying to kill someone," she said. "You look downright lethal."

He froze in mid-cut, but didn't look up. "It's a special technique I learned when I was training at Gonsalves in Japan. It—um—helps keep the lettuce from bruising."

"I had no idea you could bruise lettuce," she said, trailing the tip of her finger around the rim of her glass. "Amazing, the things you learn. Are the boys sleeping?"

Shit, a *normal mom* would have thought to ask long before this. She should probably check on them—

"They bounced themselves to sleep in those little chairs,

so I put them in their cribs," Sam said, dumping the lettuce in a bowl before reaching for a tomato. "Their morning nap was a little earlier than the usual routine, so it seemed smart to slip in another one now."

"They're champion nappers. I can't believe how much they sleep. I think they get it from their father."

"You spoken with him lately?"

"No," she said, feeling a pang of guilt about the ignored messages. Technically, she hadn't spoken with him. Still, the calls were becoming relentless, as were the demands they get back together as a family.

"Sheridan, a responsible *parent would want her children to have both a father and a mother,"* he'd growled in his last voicemail.

She'd erased the message, wishing she could erase the guilt and worry building in the back of her mind.

She studied Sam, wondering if it bothered him to be caring for another man's kids. Probably not. He wasn't like the macho military guys she'd been around. The guys who wouldn't dream of diapering their own children, let alone someone else's.

"I can give them their baths later," he said. "After they wake up."

"It's fine if they miss it once in a while, right? I mean, they're babies. It's not like they're going on a date and need to impress anyone. That should be okay, right?"

Sam looked up, then nodded wisely. "Absolutely. That's what it says in all the childrearing books."

"I figured. They handled it okay after I left this morning?"

"They did. There was a little crying, but I stopped after about an hour."

Sheri laughed, soothed by his sense of humor in spite of her guilt pangs over leaving the boys. She had to work—not just to keep a roof over their heads, but for her own sanity. Still, there were moments she feared every choice she made had the potential to damage the boys for life.

Sam dumped the tomato into the bowl, then reached for an avocado. He held it up for a moment, studying it like he wasn't entirely sure what to do with it. Probably considering the proper kind of cut, whether he should do it rondelle or chiffonade or one of those other fancy techniques she'd only read about in cookbooks. She bit her lip, wishing she could be more useful.

"Want me to do it?" she asked, standing up. "I have this cute little avocado cutter my ex-mother-in-law gave me before she realized I was a total disaster in the kitchen."

"Avocado cutter?"

"It's silly, but it works."

She scooted around him, then bent down to rummage through the lower drawer. It took her a moment to find it, and she had to paw through at least a dozen other abandoned kitchen tools she'd bought with the hope of being a better cook.

When she stood up, he was staring with his mouth slightly open.

Whoops. Had she shown off more than her avocado peeler when she'd bent down?

"Here," she said, plucking the plump avocado from his fingers as she tried to ignore her flaming cheeks. "I can finish this if you want to get the rest of the food plated."

"Of course," he said, brushing past her en route to the silverware drawer. The kitchen was small, and Sam was not, so his hard, chiseled frame pressed into her as he moved to grab napkins and silverware.

"Pardon me," he said, brushing against her as he slipped past on his way to the fridge. "More wine?"

"I'm good for now," she said, gasping a little as he brushed against her again, electricity sparking everywhere they made contact. She finished slicing the avocado and tossed it into the bowl, then remembered a great vinaigrette she'd grabbed at the grocery store a week ago and shoved in the upper cupboard for when she ran out.

She stretched up to reach it, her T-shirt riding up above the waistband of her skirt as she felt around for the bottle.

"Here, let me," Sam said, moving behind her to reach over her head. "Which one?"

His body pressed hot and solid against hers, hard in all the right places. She gasped, afraid to move or even breathe, certain she was going to explode with desire or simply melt back against him and beg him to touch her.

"White bottle," she squeaked. "Brown polka dots."

He shifted a little, grazing her backside with the fly of his shorts. Was it her imagination, or was there something hard jutting against her tailbone?

"Got it." He lowered his arm, and Sheri turned, bringing them face-to-face in the cramped little kitchen. His breath ruffled her hair, and she breathed in the scent of kitchen spices and dish soap and hot, delicious man. Sam swallowed, and she watched his Adam's apple move, watched a flicker of something spark in his eyes.

"Here you go," he breathed, swallowing again. "Need anything else?"

God, yes.

She took the bottle from him, gripping it hard to keep from grabbing him. "That's it. Thanks."

"You're welcome," he said, and stepped away.

Heat surged through her as she finished tossing the salad with the dressing, wondering if this was all in her imagination, or if he was feeling it too. God, she hadn't been this discombobulated by a man for years. Maybe ever. Her whole body buzzed with heat and desire and flat-out lust for the man now folding napkins into place at her dining room table.

She turned and took three steps into the dining area, her hip brushing his arm as she bent to fill his salad bowl. She thought she saw him lift his finger as if to touch the edge of her skirt, and even though she knew it was a bad idea, she grazed him with her breast when she leaned down to retrieve a piece of wayward tomato she'd dropped on the floor.

At last, she settled into her seat, folded her napkin in her lap, and picked up her wineglass. They were seated at opposite ends of the table, their plates brimming with food, their minds brimming with lust.

Or maybe that's just me, she thought, taking a sip of wine.

Across the table, Sam lifted his glass.

"So," he began. "Are you *trying* to drive me insane, or do you genuinely want me to throw you across this table and fuck you 'til neither of us can stand?"

Chapter Ten

As Sam whacked Sheri on the back, trying to get her to stop choking on her wine, it occurred to him he needed to work on his communication skills.

"Sorry," he said, giving her one more solid thump as she blinked up at him through teary eyes. "I probably could have broached the subject better."

"*You think*?" she gasped.

"Just trying to get a handle on the elephant in the room."

She coughed again and gave him an incredulous look. "By shooting it with a grenade launcher instead of a tranquilizer dart?"

He grinned as he handed her back into her chair and returned to his seat a safe distance away. He shrugged and picked up his fork. "Why use a big gun when a bigger one will do?"

"I really don't think we should be talking about the size of your gun," she said, stabbing into her salad with more force than necessary. "The last thing I need right now is a man in my life or in my bed or in my—in my—"

She trailed off, looking flustered as she forked a bite of salad into her mouth and chewed with startling vigor.

He speared a piece of pork and held it thoughtfully for a moment. "Look, we didn't really talk about what happened last night—what almost happened—and now we're dancing around each other trying to pretend nothing's going on between us. I just think we need to get this out in the open."

She took a sip of wine, regarding him coolly over the rim of her glass. "And what, pray tell, do you think is going on?"

"I'm insanely hot for you. In case that wasn't painfully obvious."

"It wasn't, but thank you for clarifying." Her cheeks flushed a lovely shade of pink, and he watched as she raised the napkin to her lips.

"And based on the way you were squirming and pressing up against me last night," he said, "I get the sense you aren't exactly repulsed by me."

She shrugged and looked up at the ceiling. "You're not hideous."

He speared a piece of tomato and tried not to look at her breasts. "But I think we both know that acting on our urges wouldn't be smart."

"Of course."

"I work for you. Well, I work for Mac, and obviously he makes the rules here. Either way, it's a conflict of interest. A very clear violation of ethics and laws and codes and—"

"Wait a minute. My brother told you not to sleep with me, didn't he?" She set her fork down, looking annoyed.

"What?"

"Argh! That is *so* like him. Dammit, now I want to fuck you just to get him back."

This time, it was Sam's turn to choke on his wine. She started to stand, probably looking to whack him on the back in revenge, but he waved her off. When he stopped coughing, he shook his head.

"That doesn't seem like the best reason to have sex with someone," he said stupidly.

"No? Well, how about the fact that I *want* to jump your bones?"

"That's a good reason."

She set down her wineglass. "I'm not saying I'm going to. That would be the dumbest thing ever. I need a nanny, not a gigolo. I'm barely getting my life back together right now with this move and this job and this house. It would be insane to fuck the person who's helping me do it all."

"Well put." He swallowed, not certain where to go with the conversation from here. "Okay, so we both agree that sleeping together wouldn't be smart."

"Agreed." She frowned. "Wait, are you saying that because you're not attracted to me, or because—"

"Sheri, Jesus." He raked his hands through his hair. "Look, I want nothing more than to lift your skirt to palm that incredible ass, bend you over the kitchen counter, and make you scream my name. But I've seen your brother double-tap a moving target in high winds from 400 meters while running across cobblestones, and since I value my life—"

"When did you see my brother shoot?"

He froze. He gripped his fork, struggling to regain control of himself and this conversation.

"At a shooting range," he said. "In college."

"They have cobblestones at shooting ranges?"

"It was a very specialized shooting range."

"Whatever," she said, and speared a piece of avocado with more force than necessary. "I talked with Kelli this afternoon about how close I came to sleeping with you last night, and she said—"

"You told your friend *that*?"

"Of course. What do you think women talk about, pedicures and feelings?"

He swallowed. "Isn't Kelli friends with Mac?"

Sheri rolled her eyes as she finished chewing a bite of salad. "No. Kelli wants to jump Mac, but he's not aware she exists. That's something I'd like to change in the future, but we're getting off-topic here. So we're in agreement about not sleeping together?"

He hesitated, then nodded. "Absolutely."

Sheri lifted her wineglass. "Okay then. Here's to a platonic, professional, completely sexless working relationship."

"Cheers," he said, lifting his glass to hers.

It was the lousiest toast he'd ever made.

• • •

Sam did his best to avoid Sheri for the rest of the evening. That meant staying out of the kitchen, since she was out there banging pots and pans and doing something involving the blender.

He hid out in his bedroom, thankful he had a private bathroom so he could bathe the twins without running into her in the hallway. If he was going to keep his word—both to her and to Mac—it was wise to minimize temptation.

After bath time, he set the boys on a blanket on his floor and demonstrated a series of low-crawl drills and military push-ups.

"You want your hands shoulder-width apart like this for the push-up," he said to Jackson, maneuvering the baby into position. Jackson giggled and grabbed hold of Sam's finger with a surprisingly fierce grip.

"Excellent." He saluted both boys. "Starting position— hut! I'll call cadence. Ready? One, two, three."

Jeffrey rolled over and attempted to stick his own foot in his mouth. Jackson screeched and crawled two feet before flopping on his belly and smacking his hand in a puddle of his own drool.

Sam smiled. "I had a buddy in the Marines who used to do that after a night of bar crawling. Not the sort of crawling you should be doing, incidentally."

Jackson gave him a drooly grin and farted.

"Atta boy," Sam said, and patted him on the back. "Probably good we're hiding out in here if we're doing guy stuff like that. If you want to scratch yourself inappropriately, now's the time."

Jeffrey smacked his pudgy palm on Sam's pocket, which held his phone, wallet, and a pocketknife. Sam pulled it all out and set everything safely on the dresser, out of the boys' reach.

"That reminds me, I need to Google culinary knife techniques," Sam muttered. "I probably shouldn't have used my dive knife to make salad. Now your mom thinks I look more like I'm prepping for hand-to-hand combat than prepping lettuce."

Which was pretty much true, but it was bad to be so transparent. Between forgetting the diaper bag, burning the brisket, making the beds with military precision when he knew not to, screwing up the knife thing, and sticking his foot in his mouth over dinner, he wasn't exactly batting a thousand today.

"Gotta be more careful," he told the babies. "I owe it to your uncle. And your mom. She made it pretty clear she's not interested in swapping spit with military guys after what your daddy pulled."

Especially not one who lied to her the way Sam was doing.

The boys bounced up and down a few times and made some fussy noises he feared could be the start of another crying jag. He stood up and scooped one baby into each arm, savoring the sweet warmth of them cradled against his chest. "Come on. Time for bed."

He put the boys down quietly, careful to avoid Sheri out in the kitchen. He heard her moving around in the boys' room several times over the next few minutes, so he knew she was checking on them. At one point, he thought he heard Kelli's voice down the hall, followed by the whirring of the blender. *Margaritas,* he thought, and wished he had one. A margarita sounded good, but not good enough to brave a trip down the hall and the temptation of Sheri's pantyless ass curving beneath her skirt. Better to stay here at the other end of the house with his pants safely zipped.

En route from his bedroom to check on the boys, he spotted Sheri's iPhone in a basket on the hall table. Glancing around to make sure she wasn't watching, he flicked the power button and looked down at the screen. A text message flashed up at him.

Why the fuck aren't you answering my calls? Don't make me do something drastic, Sheri.

Sam scowled. The sender was Jonathan Price. How long had he been trying to contact her? What the hell did he want?

He started to scroll for past messages, but footsteps from the kitchen signaled Sheri was on the move. He powered the phone off and put it back, slipping quietly back into his room.

So Limpdick was harassing her. He'd have to check the phone again later. It was Sam's job to keep him away. To protect this family. To protect *her*. He needed to check in with Mac, to let him know things were escalating.

Back in his room, Sam fired off an e-mail to Mac and one to his sisters letting them know he was okay. After that, he played a few rounds of darts with the small dartboard he'd tacked to one of the ridiculous apricot walls. His aim was still true, which was a small comfort. Not that he planned to return to his life as a sniper, but at least he still had the skills.

An hour later, Sam stared at his empty water glass. Even with the air-conditioning, it was hot as hell in here. Or maybe that was sexual frustration. He'd already taken a cold shower in hopes of cooling his libido. Now his stupid ice water was empty.

He stepped over to the door, listening for noises from the kitchen. He didn't hear anything, so maybe she'd gone to bed. Maybe it was safe to brave the journey down the hall.

Since when are you such a chickenshit?

Sam sighed and unlocked his bedroom door. It wasn't a matter of that. It was about respecting Sheri's boundaries.

It was about honoring his commitment to a friend. About following through on what he said he'd do. About remembering that the last time he'd failed to do something he pledged to do, innocent men had died. Horrible, awful deaths that could have been prevented if only Sam had done what his commanding officer ordered him to.

He gripped his water glass harder, fighting to block the memories as he made his way down the hall. Screams still echoed in his head, and he saw the flash of fire, felt the thunderous blast, felt the wave of scorching heat.

God, would he ever forget?

He shook his head, rounding the corner to the kitchen.

He froze in the doorway, paralyzed by what he saw.

Blood.

Blood everywhere—on the floor, on the counter, *Jesus*, even on the ceiling. And glass, holy shit, shards of glass everywhere.

And at the center of it all, Sheri.

Sheri with her hands and face and clothes and arms covered in red spatter, and a horrified look on her face.

"No!"

Chapter Eleven

Sheri froze as Sam's shout echoed in her ear. She opened her mouth to say something, but he lunged for her. His hands were everywhere at once, patting her throat, stroking her arms, touching her face—

"Oh, God—*no!*" he said.

Oh, yes! screamed Sheri's whole body as his hands slid down her torso.

She raised her hands and pushed them against his wall of a chest, reluctant to lose contact with him, but needing ease his panic.

"Sam, stop! I'm okay. Please, stop."

She stepped back, wincing as a piece of glass bit into her heel. "Ouch!" she said, and lifted her bare foot to inspect the damage. It didn't look bloody, but it was tough to tell with so much beet pulp sprayed around the kitchen.

"Damn beets," she muttered, flicking a piece off the edge of her big toe before setting her foot back on the floor.

"Beets," he said slowly, and Sheri watched as his expression went from horror to confusion to relief, all in the space of two seconds. "Beets. Not blood?"

"Of course not blood. Jesus, did you think I was butchering an elk in here?"

"But I thought you were hit."

"Hit?"

"Shot. All this blood and glass and—"

"Yeah, I'm going to need a new blender." She rolled her eyes and waved a hand toward what was left of her Black & Decker. "Note to self: don't stick a metal spoon in a glass blender while it's running. Any idea how to get beet pulp off the ceiling?"

He blinked at her, still looking dumbfounded. Then he glanced up, and Sheri directed her gaze skyward as well. A chunk of beet lost its grip on the ceiling and dropped down the front of her shirt with a splat.

She sighed. "*Normal moms* would know how to make homemade baby food without destroying a kitchen."

"What?"

She shook her head and reached down the front of her shirt to fish the beet out of her bra. After dropping it in the garbage disposal, she rinsed off her hand with a sense of defeat.

"I read this article about how beets make great baby food because they're colorful and packed with calcium and potassium and vitamin A. Kelli got a bunch of them on sale at the farmers' market by her house, so I thought I could steam them and blend them into this great organic baby food." She shrugged and wiped a hunk of beet off her arm. "The story of my life."

"Your life," Sam choked out. "Jesus, I'm just glad you're okay. I don't care about the damn kitchen, that's easy to clean."

She gave him a halfhearted smile and pulled a piece of beet out of her hair. "Easy for you to say, Martha Stewart."

"Seriously. You almost gave me a heart attack. Let me clean this up while you go take a shower."

"No!" she said, staving off a fresh wave of shame. "I made this mess, and I didn't even get any baby food out of it. The least I can do is clean it up."

She took a step toward the sink and winced, glancing down at her beet-stained bare foot. "Dammit, the glass is everywhere. I just need to—"

He slung an arm around her waist, picking her up like she weighed less than a bag of palm fronds. She squirmed against him, but he locked his other arm around her, gripping her tight against his chest.

"The only thing you need to do is take a shower so you don't look like the victim of a shrapnel explosion," he said, carrying her toward the door of the kitchen. "The mess will wait. Or you'll swallow your goddamn pride and let someone else help you for a change. Either way, you're getting in the shower right now."

Sheri pushed at his chest, not sure if she wanted to break free or just to touch him. It didn't really matter, since the solid plane of muscle resisting her hand was clearly not budging.

"Put me down!" she demanded.

He ignored her, striding through the dining room and down the hall, making a beeline for her bedroom. He kicked open the door, stepping over her discarded robe and panties en route to the master bath. He loosened his grip on her for an instant, just enough to twist the taps for the shower.

"Sam, stop it! Just let me clean up the mess, and then I'll—"

"This isn't negotiable," he said, perching her on the edge of the bathroom counter with one hand holding her in place. He held fast to her rib cage while the other hand moved down her beet-stained calf. She gasped with the pleasure of his palm on her skin, then yelped as he grabbed her foot.

"Ow!"

"Exactly," he said, clutching her heel in one massive palm. "You've got glass in your foot and you're bleeding all over the place. You're going to get cleaned up and bandaged, and that's happening whether you want it to or not. We can do this the hard way, or we can do this the easy way. Your choice."

She winced as he plucked a piece of glass from her heel, then another one up near the ball of her foot. He flicked them into the sink and ran water to wash away the small shards. Then he opened her medicine cabinet and located a bottle of antibacterial rinse, setting it on the counter long enough to scrounge a Q-tip from the jar beside the sink.

She said nothing as he grabbed her foot again, bending over his work as he tended to the tiny wounds.

"There," he said. "I think I got all the glass. Wash off in the shower, and we'll take another look afterward to see if there's more. Then I'll put a bandage on it."

"But I'm already covered in beet juice. Just let me clean up the kitchen now while I'm a mess, and then I'll come back here and—"

"Goddamn it." He grabbed her around the waist, hoisting

her off the counter with a quick jerk.

Startled, she braced herself as he thrust her into the tiled shower. She gasped as the warm spray hit her, stunned to be standing in the shower in her clothes while some Neanderthal gripped her around the rib cage.

Sam grabbed the hem of her shirt and tugged up. Too shocked to resist, she lifted her arms and let him pull off her drenched, beet-stained T-shirt while the water pounded her from above.

She blinked as he tossed aside the shirt, his eyes pinning her in place as she stood there in her pink satin bra made transparent by the water. Her nipples tightened as he grabbed the waistband of her skirt.

He hesitated, probably realizing he'd crossed at least a dozen lines they'd sworn they wouldn't get near. He started to draw his hand back, but Sheri grabbed his wrist and gripped it tight. Her fingers locked around his hand, and her eyes locked with his. She watched as his eyes went from flashing anger to mild alarm.

Good.

Her belly rolled with a surge of triumph and dizzying lust, and she let go of his hand and slid her palm down the plane of his abdomen, grabbing the top of his shorts. She jerked him to her, catching him off guard. Sam stumbled, tripping forward into the tiled shower, into *her.*

It was his turn to be shocked as the warm spray hit him squarely in the face. He was still sputtering when she grabbed the neck of his T-shirt shirt and yanked his face down to hers.

"You said we can do this the hard way," she purred, grazing her breasts against his chest. "Show me you're a man of your word."

He swallowed, closing his eyes for the briefest instant before opening them to look down at her.

"My pleasure," he said, and pushed her against the slick tile wall.

Chapter Twelve

Keep your hands off my sister.

Mac's words were a distant buzz in the back of Sam's brain, something faint and hollow and not entirely human.

The woman in his arms—Sheri, with her arms twined around his neck and her breasts pressed against his chest—she was all human. All woman. And all his, at least for the moment.

He watched her panting with need and hesitated. He could still walk away now, stick with the agreement they'd made only hours before. It was the right thing to do, especially knowing how much she'd hate him if she knew who he really was. Why he was really here.

He started to pull back.

Sheri grabbed his arm. "Please," she begged, her voice raspy with lust and steam from the shower. "I want you. Just this once."

She didn't have to ask twice. Hell, she didn't need to ask

the first time. All she had was to do exactly what she was doing now, sliding her wet hands over his arms, down his chest, clutching at the sodden fabric of his T-shirt.

He grabbed the hem and jerked it over his head, tossing it above the glass shower door so it landed with a *splat* on the other side. He reached for her again, desperate to feel her writhing wet and lush against him.

He skimmed his hands around her back, enjoying the satiny softness of her skin as he found the clasp on her bra. He fumbled a bit there, his hands shaking with urgency and desire and the powerful nature of what he was about to do. What *they* were about to do.

"*Please.*" She whimpered. "Rip it off if you have to. I want to feel you."

Sam gave a mighty tug and the bra came apart. He had no idea whether he'd ripped the fabric or just forced the clasp into submission, but he didn't care. He dropped the bra to the floor and kicked it aside, groaning as he lowered his mouth to her exposed breasts. She gasped and gripped his hair, pulling him against her as she arched to meet him.

"*Yes,*" she hissed as he sucked hard on her nipple, drawing it into his mouth and devouring it with his tongue. He grazed her with his teeth, then turned gentle again with a series of soft licks and warm breaths against her skin. She was moaning low in her throat, gripping his hair so hard he expected to see clumps of it washing down the drain.

He moved to the other breast, licking, sucking, nipping as he brushed his hands down her back to cup that magnificent ass through her wet skirt. She arched willingly, pressing herself against the fly of his shorts.

He palmed her ass, stroking and rubbing through the

soaked cotton, aware that there was nothing beneath it but Sheri. Only Sheri. He drew back and looked down at her, his breath catching in his throat at the heat in her eyes.

"Too many clothes," he said, clutching the wet fabric bunched around her hips.

"Any ideas how to fix that?" she breathed, giving him a coy smile.

"One or two."

He tugged down, dropping to his knees in front of her as he pulled the wet fabric over her thighs, down her beautiful calves and into a wet puddle at her feet. He stayed kneeling before her with the water pounding his skull and her fingers still clenched in his hair.

He moved his palms up her calves, then over her knees and up her thighs, parting them gently as he breathed against her silky skin. Cupping her ass, he pulled her so close he could almost taste her.

"I thought of you earlier," she said.

He looked up, admiring the undersides of her breasts. "What?"

"Before dinner. I touched myself and thought of you."

The words went straight to his throbbing hard-on. He planted a slow kiss at the top of her pubic bone, then another an inch lower. She moaned as he moved even lower.

"What did you think about?"

"This," she gasped, gripping the back of his head. "This."

He tasted her then, tentatively at first, then like a starving man with an ice cream cone. He dipped his tongue into her, probing, licking, devouring. She cried out, squirming against him as she gripped the back of his head with a fierceness that surprised him.

She was dripping wet, and he knew it wasn't just the shower. He flattened his tongue, making broad strokes that covered every inch of her flesh. Her whimpers were growing louder now, and he let go of her ass with one hand and moved it slowly around, gliding up her inner thigh.

He slipped one finger into her, awestruck by the hot wetness of her. She gasped as he slid another finger inside, moving deep into her when she cried out again. He kept his tongue on her swollen clit, circling faster now.

"Don't stop!" she gasped. "Oh, God."

He felt her clench around his finger, felt her whole body go rigid. Then she spasmed around him, a tight, rhythmic squeeze that left him wondering what she'd feel like wrapped around something other than his fingers.

He licked her again, faster this time, more rhythmically. She bucked and tensed and called out his name, twisting her fingers in his hair.

When she finally went still, she released her grip on his hair. Her cries subsided, replaced by soft breathing and the spatter of water on the tile floor. Sam planted a kiss at the top of her right thigh, then another on her left hip bone as he stood up, his own legs a little shaky. He held her around the waist in case she toppled.

She looked at him through hooded eyes, her cheeks flushed and damp. Her hair was plastered to her throat and shoulders, and her panting breaths made her breasts rise and fall in a tantalizing motion.

"Thank you," she whispered, then smiled at him.

"You're welcome," he said, planting a kiss on her forehead. "Do you need to rest now or—"

"Are you kidding?" She grabbed his waistband and fixed

her fingers around his zipper, giving him a wicked grin. "I'm not even close to done with you."

She tugged the zipper and fumbled the button open, then shoved down his shorts and underwear. They fell to his feet and Sam kicked them away, gasping as her fingers circled him. She stroked gently at first, testing him, adjusting her grip. She quickened her pace, stroking, squeezing, her fingers deft and hot.

He gritted his teeth and closed his eyes, letting his head fall back against the shower wall. She stroked him faster, her fingers moving expertly as she bent down and flicked her tongue over the tip of him. Sam felt his heart rip away from his chest and felt certain he'd die happy if he passed out right now.

"I want you inside me," she whispered, her breath soft on his shaft. "Right now."

He swallowed and opened his eyes, knowing there was no way he could possibly tell her no, but also knowing he couldn't be completely stupid.

"I don't have any—"

"Condoms?" she asked, rising up to lick her way over his belly, across his chest. Her fingers still stroked him in a rhythm he knew would have him teetering over the edge in about ten seconds.

"Medicine cabinet. Kelli put them there the day you arrived."

Sam raised an eyebrow, then stepped out of the shower. "Kelli was planning ahead?" He popped open the cabinet and grabbed the box, his eyes skimming over the wording. "Super-magnum-jumbo?"

"She hadn't actually met you when she bought them,"

she said, dropping her eyes to his crotch, "but obviously there won't be any problems with the fit."

"You're making my head swell."

She gave him a devilish grin as she pulled him back into the shower and pried the condom from his hand. "That's sorta the idea."

She stroked him again, putting on the condom with expert hands. Her words became a distant buzz in his ears, smothered by the thought of being inside her, of holding her around the waist and plunging in deep and losing himself completely.

He gripped her hips and hoisted her up, pinning her against the shower wall. Her breath caught, and she smiled, urging him, daring him to do it. He knew he should take his time, should go slow. She was a new mom, sweet, vulnerable. His best friend's sister.

But there was no way to hold back. No way to stop himself from taking her fast and hard and deep.

She saw the look in his eye and gave him a devilish smile.

"*Yes*," she whispered. "Take me now. *Please.*"

He plunged into her, all shreds of restraint falling away. He moaned as she sheathed him, wet, tight, and warm around him as he drove himself into her. He drew back, thinking there was still time to slow things down, to make sure she was okay, that *they* were okay.

"Again!" she cried, squirming to force him deeper.

He gripped her thighs and plunged into her again, then again and again and again. She shrieked his name, hissing words in his ear that he never imagined a sweet mother of two would know, much less beg him to do as he drove into her over and over, pushing them both toward the edge of the cliff.

"Sheri," he groaned. "I can't—"

"Do it," she gasped, and he did.

Electrified waves of pleasure hit him as he thrust deeper, burying himself inside her, losing himself completely as she cried out, giving in to her own shudders of pleasure. She clenched around him, squeezing, grinding, matching him thrust for thrust as she called his name over and over.

Everything went dark in Sam's brain. Pitch black, no light at all. Or maybe he'd lost his vision. Or maybe—

"The power's out," Sheri whispered, slipping down his hips and detaching their bodies with more haste than he expected. "It happens sometimes on the island. I should make sure the boys are okay."

Sam nodded, not sure he could manage to breathe, much less walk down the hall and peer over the edge of a crib. His eyes were adjusting to the darkness, and he could make out the faint shape of her silhouette. "Power. Right. Definitely. I'll be right there."

Sheri laughed and patted him on the butt, then pirouetted under the shower spray, smoothing her hair back. "I'm all clean. Looks like you managed to fuck all the beet off me."

"There's a phrase I've never heard after sex."

She laughed again, then twirled under the spray once more before hopping out of the shower and grabbing a fluffy towel off the hook by the door. She lit a lone candle on the counter, giving him a better view of her damp, naked body. The candlelight gave everything a soft, dreamy glow, and Sam felt certain he'd never been this happy after sex.

She toweled herself off, smiling at him as she bent down to dry her legs, looking so beautiful and warm and fuckable he wanted her all over again.

Just as soon as he got feeling back in his legs.

"What's that tattoo on your shoulder?" she asked, rubbing the towel through her hair. "I can't see it in this light."

Sam did a mental cringe and turned so his back was to her. "It's nothing. Just something I got when I was a lot younger."

"Can I look at it?"

"Maybe later," he said, grabbing a towel off the bar beside the shower and pulling it over his shoulders. He angled away and began drying his hair, careful to keep the terry cloth over the telltale mark.

Sheri studied him a moment, her expression somewhere between wariness and intrigue. Sam gave her a reassuring smile. He draped the towel over his shoulders and bent to kiss her.

"You're amazing," he said. "You know that? I knew you were beautiful back when I was a dumb college student with too much testosterone and you were this goddess in a white bikini, but now—" He shook his head, at a loss for words. "I didn't expect you to be like this."

"Like what?"

"So sweet and funny and sexy and smart and caring and sexy and clever and kind and sexy and—Christ, I sound like a fucking Hallmark card." He shook his head. "I'm not good at this stuff."

She blinked, her eyes suddenly damp. "I think you're doing pretty well."

"Did I mention sexy?"

"Maybe once or twice."

She stood on tiptoe to kiss him, a softer, gentler kiss than they'd shared just moments before. When she dropped back on her heels, she looked at him for several beats without saying a word.

"You're amazing."

"So are you."

She smiled and turned away. "I'm going to go check on the boys," she called as she padded into the bedroom and emerged a few seconds later with the purple robe draped around her. "Take your time getting dressed."

The lights popped back on, and he felt a bit of the romantic afterglow drain away. Sheri glanced up at the ceiling, then back at Sam. "Guess the power's back on."

"Guess so."

They locked eyes for a moment and Sam tried to read what was there. Regret? Joy? A little of both?

"Okay then," she said, stepping back. "I'll go look in on the boys."

"Sheri, wait."

But she was gone, off to do what she pleased, never mind his orders. Sheri was not the sort of woman to be bossed around, and Sam had to admire that. Besides, what was he going to say? *That was a mistake? That was the best sex of my life?* Both were probably true, but neither seemed quite right.

He rinsed off in a hurry, grabbing a second green towel and patting himself dry before wrapping it around his waist. He blew out the candle she'd left behind, wondering if they should talk or snuggle or just pretend this hadn't happened. What was the etiquette here?

He moved out of the bathroom and down the hall, wondering where she'd left her cell phone. He wanted to check for more messages, to see if Limpdick had been in touch again. He needed to call Mac and make sure he'd seen the e-mail about Limpdick's text message.

"Sheri?" he called. "Where are you?"

"I'm out here," she yelled back, but her voice sounded faint. Nervous. Sam felt the hair rise on the back of his neck as he glanced quickly into the babies' room, relieved to see they were both sleeping soundly.

Still, something wasn't right. He could feel it.

"Sheri?"

"I'm out here. At the front door. And, um, Sam?"

"Yeah?"

"There's someone here you need to meet."

Chapter Thirteen

Sheri breathed deeply, on the brink of hyperventilating. She fought to calm her jangling nerves while buying herself some time to figure out how the hell to handle the most awkward situation she'd encountered since the day she'd shown up at her Mommy and Me group with thong panties static-glued to her sweatshirt.

She blinked, her eyes still adjusting the darkness. The porch light was dim, but she could still see that familiar, handsome face staring coolly back at her.

"Jonathan," she said at last.

It was partly to warn Sam, who'd come into the room behind her, and partly to remind herself of her ex-husband's name. She realized her hand hurt and glanced at it, then released her death grip on the door and watched the blood drain back into her fingers. She turned back to her visitor and regarded him through the rusty screen door.

"What the hell are you doing here?"

"Sheridan," he said, brushing invisible dust off the immaculate sleeve of his navy whites. "Is that the most polite greeting you can manage for the father of your children?"

Sheri felt her skin prickle with disgust, and wondered where Sam had left that weird-looking chef's knife. She imagined plunging it into Jonathan's chest, then forced herself to take three deep breaths before speaking. "Be grateful I didn't slam the door in your face, you cheating, scum-sucking, low-life, spineless piece of—"

"Hi, I'm Sam."

Her half-naked manny stepped up beside her, using his broad shoulder as a shield between her and Jonathan. Sam had a towel around his waist, a sheen of water glistening across his chest, and a look that suggested he would be happy to punch a hole in the screen door and strangle Jonathan with his bare hands if Sheri gave the order.

She considered it, then decided blood was too difficult to scrub off the doorstep.

"A little late for a visit, wouldn't you say?" Sam said. His tone was casually cheerful, but the ice in his voice made Sheri shiver. Or maybe that was the memory of what the two of them had been doing just seconds before. His bare torso was inches away, and Sheri could feel the warmth radiating from his skin. She fought the urge to touch him, to lean into him and absorb all that strength and delicious heat.

"I'm sorry, who did you say you were?" Jonathan asked, folding his arms over chest. "I must have missed that."

"Sam is my manny," Sheri said, matching her ex-husband's folded arm stance. It was less an effort to look tough and more that she felt the belt on her robe slipping.

"Manny?" Jonathan asked in the same tone he would

have used to say "gigolo" or "stripper." He narrowed his eyes at Sam. "What the hell is a manny?"

"A male nanny," Sam supplied. "Often utilized in a caretaker capacity to provide domestic support and a positive male role model in situations where the paternal figure has abandoned his familial obligations."

Jonathan blinked, trying to figure out if he'd just been insulted. "What?" He snorted. "Did you see that on *Oprah*?"

"*The View*, actually," Sam said, his tone eerily cheerful. "It was an episode discussing the idea of whether men who cheat on their wives and abandon their infant sons should be castrated or publicly stoned."

"I must have missed that episode," Sheri said, edging her body between the two men in case one decided to lunge for the other. "Let me repeat the question, Jonathan—why are you here?"

"Haven't you gotten my messages? I've been trying to reach you. I think it's time we stop this nonsense and get back together. It's the right thing to do for the boys."

Sheri blinked, digesting his words the way she imagined she'd digest a piece of rotting meat. "Are you out of your fucking mind?"

Jonathan frowned. "For crying out loud, Sheridan. I hope you don't speak to our children using that sort of profanity."

"Oh, that's rich. The guy who abandoned his wife and newborn twins for a *stripper* suddenly gives a shit about their well-being?"

Jonathan regarded her with a familiar steely look that made the hair prickle on her arms. "We need to talk," he said. "I'm leaving for my new command in ten days. Naples. Remember how we used to talk about going to Italy? There are joint jobs there. If we're going to rekindle things between us, I really think —"

"You're not thinking at all, Jonathan. Not sanely, anyway. You're supposed to call if you want to see the boys."

"I did call," he replied icily. "About an hour ago. Was there a reason you didn't answer your phone?" He raised an eyebrow at her through the rusted screen, and Sheri resisted the urge to unfold her arms and cinch the belt on her robe.

"I left my phone in the kitchen. That's none of your business anyway," she snapped. "And if you refer to the conditions of our divorce paperwork and custody agreement, you're required to provide twenty-four hours' notice if you want to see the boys."

"This is ridiculous, Sheridan. I shouldn't have to make an appointment to see my wife and kids."

"I'm *not* your wife," she snapped. "And you sure as hell haven't had any interest in seeing the boys the last seven months. You hightailed it out of here before they could even sit up."

"You're exaggerating. I would think someone concerned with their kids' well-being would be more focused on staying levelheaded when dealing with the only father they have. I know what's best for this family, Sheridan. For *you.*"

Sheri gripped the edge of the door again, imagining it as his skull with her fingers digging into his eye sockets. She hated how hurt and betrayed she felt even now, staring down the man who'd pledged "for better or worse" and then fled the first chance he got. She swallowed hard, fighting back the threat of tears.

Beside her, Sam inched closer and rested a hand in the small of her back. "I think it's time for you to go now, Price."

Jonathan narrowed his eyes at Sam before turning back to Sheri. "You need to let this go. The thing with Candy just happened, but if you look at the big picture of what's best here—"

"You *just happened* to trip over your shoelaces and fall with your dick in another woman?" Sheri snapped. "You *just happened* to forget you had a wife and kids? You *just happened* to decide not to come home one day? Spare me, you lying piece of shit. You don't know what's best for anyone but yourself."

A hint of alarm flickered over Sam's face, and Sheri grimaced at the shrewish sound of her own voice. But goddammit, she was pissed. She had a right to her feelings, didn't she?

Jonathan shook his head. "I suppose Saint Sheridan has never been swayed by emotion and ended up doing something passionate and impulsive? Come on, Sheri. Kids need to have their mother and father together. Don't you want to do the right thing for our children?"

Sheri took a step back as the twin barbs found their mark. She bumped against Sam's chest and felt him hard and warm against her spine. The sound of his voice startled her.

"You heard what the lady told you," Sam said, his words tipped with ice. "I suggest you leave now and come back at a more reasonable time for a visit. If you want to see the boys, you need to phone Sheri and adhere to the terms of the custody agreement. Until then, don't show up here unannounced again. Is that clear?"

Jonathan narrowed his eyes at Sam, then flicked them dismissively over Sheri. "This isn't over."

Sam glared back, radiating danger. "It most certainly is." He shut the door in his face.

Sheri shivered. Sam looked down at her, concern etched on his features.

"Are you okay?"

"I'm fine. Just angry. Really, really angry."

"I understand. Why didn't you tell me he'd been harassing you?"

She looked away, feeling guilty. "It wasn't harassing, exactly. Just some phone calls and text messages. I didn't think he'd show up here."

"Now that he has, I don't want you here alone. Not ever. I understand if you need to let him see the boys, but I'm going to be here supervising."

"It's not your job description to be *my* babysitter."

He shook his head. "Are you kidding? Taking care of you and the boys is exactly my job description. Sheri, what if I hadn't been here tonight? What if he'd forced his way in?"

She shivered again, not meeting Sam's gaze. "I don't think he'd do that."

"I've known guys like him. He's not going to take no for an answer. Not from you, anyway. He needs to hear it from me. Firmly."

He looked so big and dangerous standing there in her foyer with the moonlight glinting on his torso through the window. Sheri felt her mouth go dry.

"I can't ask you to deal with my asshole ex," she said. "It's my problem, I should be the one to deal with it."

He shook his head. "Do you *ever* let someone else help you?"

She frowned and toed a spot on the carpet. "No."

"Try it sometime," he said, putting his hands on her shoulders and turning her around. "Like right now, for instance." He began marching her toward her bedroom, his hands firm and commanding and so stupidly sexy, she almost tripped over her feet.

"Sam, I don't—"

"Enough! You're going to bed. You have a long day at work tomorrow, and you need to rest. I'm going to clean up the kitchen. *You* are going to get a good night's sleep."

"But—"

"No buts. This is how it's going to be, whether you willingly accept help or if I have to tie you to your bed."

She shivered a little at his words and turned to face him in her doorway. She gave him a tentative smile. "Is this your way of avoiding the awkward conversation?"

"What awkward conversation?"

"The one that begins, 'We shouldn't have done that' and ends with 'It'll never happen again.'"

Part of her wanted him to argue—to insist it should have happened, and it ought to happen again.

Instead, he nodded. "Right."

She nodded to herself as though affirming her own words in her mind. Then she looked up at him and offered a small smile. "Good night. And thank you. For everything."

She turned and walked into her bedroom, the word *everything* echoing in her brain.

• • •

Sam spent an hour cleaning, careful not to bang cupboards or make any noise that might disturb Sheri or the boys.

The quiet gave him plenty of time to consider the fact that Limpdick had finally made contact. That he'd escalated beyond threatening text messages and had actually shown up in person to reclaim her. Every molecule of Sam's being was on alert, ready to do whatever it took to protect Sheri and her boys. This is what he'd come here to do.

You didn't come here to sleep with her.

He grimaced, recalling Mac's order for Sam to keep his hands off Sheri.

Okay, so he'd screwed that up. He'd screwed up a lot of things in his life, but he hadn't meant to let things go this far with her. What the hell had he been thinking?

He hadn't been thinking, at least not with his head. Not with *that* head. She was vulnerable. She'd made it clear she didn't want a relationship. He'd been a jerk to sleep with her, especially knowing how angry she'd be if she knew who he really was. That he'd been lying to her all along.

He gritted his teeth as he folded a dish towel. God, what if he'd ruined everything?

No. He could still get out of this. Still do his job without disappointing Mac or ruining things with Sheri. He just had to keep his distance, to make it clear to her this couldn't happen again. *Ever.*

Sam moved quietly down the hall, peering in at the boys to make sure they were still sound asleep. Then he moved to the end of the hall and looked into Sheri's room. She'd left the door ajar, and he could see her lying on her side beneath the flowered coverlet.

He felt his gut twist, and he wondered what it would be like to crawl into bed behind her, pulling her close to his chest as she tucked her backside against him and curled her body into his. He thought about breathing in the scent of her hair, feeling her breasts soft against his forearms as he held her tight to his body.

No, he told himself, and stepped away from the door. *No*.

He could still save this. He could stay up all night making sure Price didn't come back. He could stand guard over the boys, over Sheri, protecting them all. Mac never needed to know what had happened, especially if it was just a onetime thing. It never had to happen again.

He stole another glance at her sleeping form and took a deep breath. "Never again," he commanded himself, and turned to walk back to his room.

He dialed Mac's number, halfway hoping the call would go straight to voicemail.

Mac answered on the first ring. "Sam," he said crisply. "I got your e-mail about Price's text message. How's my sister?"

"Safe. Everything's fine."

"Did something happen?"

Nothing happened, Sam almost blurted, then realized Mac wasn't talking about what took place in the shower. "Lieutenant Limpdick showed up."

He proceeded to fill Mac in on Jonathan's visit, describing the exchange in excruciating detail. Mac listened quietly, a silence that could mean anything from thoughtfulness to deadly rage.

"So you think he's been in contact more than she's told you?" Mac said at last.

"I believe so. And I also don't think he's going to give up easily."

Sam started to say something else—to point out that no

man in his right mind would let someone like Sheri go so easily—but he stopped himself.

"Manipulative prick," Mac muttered. "Twenty bucks says Limpdick doesn't give a shit about seeing the boys. He just wants to get to Sheri."

"I'll make sure that doesn't happen. Should I try to get her to report Limpdick to his command?"

"She won't do it. I've suggested it before and she refused. That's a career-ender, so there's no way she'd take that step unless things really escalated."

"I'll make sure they don't."

"Thank you. I'm counting on you, Sam."

"I know," he said firmly, gripping the phone tighter. "I won't let you down."

He hoped like hell he hadn't already.

Chapter Fourteen

"I'm pretty sure my boss thinks I have diarrhea," Sheri murmured into the phone on her lunch break.

She was seated on the same log on the beach near her office, and miraculously, her stick was still right where she'd left it. She picked it up and began smoothing a flat patch in the sand.

"Hello to you, too," Kelli answered, the sound of yapping dogs echoing in the background. "Any particular reason your boss would be making assumptions about your gastrointestinal health?"

"All morning I've been making excuses to run to the bathroom so I can call Sam and check in on him and the boys."

"You say that so convincingly, I almost think you've made yourself believe it," Kelli replied. "By the way, you don't know how much I appreciated your clandestine phone call last night. Sharing the dirty details of your tryst with the manny while he cleaned your kitchen? You are the epitome of the new modern woman."

Sheri rolled her eyes and tapped her stick on the edge of the log, knocking the sand off. "I needed someone to talk to. He got kinda weird after sex."

"I can't imagine why. First your power went out, then your ex-husband showed up and acted like a menacing jerk. That would throw any guy off his stride."

"Still, he could have crawled in bed with me afterward—"

"Are you insane? With your ex in town and your brother ordering him not to touch you? I still can't believe Mac pulled that."

"Yeah, well, you know Mac."

"Not as well as I'd like to, but that's beside the point. Sam's not dumb. Besides, I thought you said you're never going to sleep with him again."

"I know, I know. You're right. Cuddling would have been a bad idea." She sighed and drove the stick back into the sand. "What did you mean about making myself believe it? Believe what?"

"That you're calling to check on the boys when you know damn well they're fine. It's Sam you're checking on."

Sheri bit her lip and considered arguing, but there was no point. Kelli was right. "You think he knows?"

"That you're hot for him? The fact that you fucked him in the shower probably gave him a pretty good idea."

"No, I mean that I'm checking on him. That I want to know what he's up to and what he's thinking about what happened last night. If he feels guilty, too."

"You know, you could try something totally crazy."

"What's that?"

"Ask him. Over dinner tonight. After the boys are in bed when you have time alone to talk."

"Talk," Sheri repeated. "About our relationship."

"Try not using that word," Kelli suggested. "It tends to scare men away. Particularly men you've only slept with once who've been threatened by your brother for doing it at all."

"Got it. Good advice. Thank you, Kel."

"You're welcome, goof. Now go eat something. You can't spend every lunch hour just gabbing with me."

"Yes, Mother," Sheri said. "Thanks again. When are you coming to dinner?"

"When your manny offers to cook it for us wearing nothing but an apron and a smile. Or when your hot brother comes for a visit. Save me some of those condoms in case that happens."

She laughed. "I'll have to check their schedules and get back to you. Thanks again, Kel."

Sheri hung up the phone and tucked it back in her purse, giving her stick one last twist in the sand. She shoved her feet back in her shoes and trudged through the parking lot where she saw the familiar old guy with a fishing pole over his shoulder.

"Afternoon, ma'am," he said, tipping his red-and-white-striped derby hat at her.

"Good afternoon," she said, smiling.

"You sure picked the prettiest spot on the beach."

"It's a good place to think," she agreed, and hurried back toward her office. She devoured a sandwich and an apple and resisted the urge to call Sam again. She didn't want to be that transparent.

She finally broke down and called during her coffee

break around two. The phone hadn't even rung yet when she heard a funny click, followed by a muffled baby giggle.

"Sam?" She pressed her ear to the phone, straining to hear what was happening. There was a scratch of fabric and something that sounded oddly like singing.

"From the halls of Montezuma to the shores of Tripoli…"

"Hello? Sam? Are you there?"

Someone was definitely singing. Sheri turned up the volume on her phone, recognizing Sam's voice at the same time she realized he'd answered the phone by mistake.

"First to fight for right and freedom, and to keep our honor clean. We are proud to claim the title of United States Marine. Our flag's unfurled to—"

"Sam? Hello?"

The singing continued, a deep baritone punctuated by giggles and squeals she recognized from her boys.

"Here's health to you and to our corps, which we are proud to serve. In many a strife we've fought for life and never lost our nerve…"

Sheri turned up the volume again, straining to hear Sam's voice and the sweet giggles of her babies. Everything sounded muffled. Was the phone in his pocket?

"If the Army and the Navy ever look on heaven's scenes, they will find the streets are guarded by United States Marines."

The singing ended in a chorus of baby squeals and shrieks of delight. Sheri bit her lip, wondering if she should just hang up the phone. But she was curious—

"Sam? Hello? Can you hear me?"

There was a rustling sound on the other end of the line, followed by Sam's voice.

"Sheri? Is that you?"

"Hi. I just called to see how the boys are doing."

"Oh. Great, they're great. Sorry, Jackson must've kicked the phone on in my pocket. I was uh—just singing them a lullaby."

"About the Marines?"

"Marines? Yes—right. That. Yeah, I had an uncle who was a Marine. He used to sing to us when we were little and—wait, how long were you on the phone?"

She stifled a giggle, stupidly charmed by the mental picture of this big, burly man singing to her children. Even if his song choice was a little odd.

"Long enough," she said. "That was the U.S. Marine Corps hymn, right? My grandpa used to sing it to me."

"Right. Yes, I think it was." There was a long pause, then the sound of a baby squealing. "Has Jonathan called to set up a time to see the boys?"

"No. I haven't heard from him."

"Which means the whole thing about seeing the boys is bullshit. It's you he wants."

Sheri bit her lip. "What I want is for him to go away and leave me alone."

"As long as I'm around, I won't let him near you or the boys unless you say it's okay."

"Thank you. I appreciate that."

"Not a problem. Just doing my job."

"Your job. Absolutely. Okay, then, I'll see you in a few hours."

She hung up fast before she could have a change of heart and decide she urgently wanted to knock boots with a man who'd sing so sweetly to her children. It was best this way, if they just pretended the whole thing never happened. They could move on with their lives maintaining a professional, platonic relationship. They may have slipped up last night, but it wouldn't happen again.

The rest of the workday crawled by, as did the drive home. By the time she pulled up the driveway, she was exhausted. She walked through the front door and set her keys on the little wooden table beside the door.

She looked down at the table, frowning. "Sam?"

"Yeah?"

"When did you build me an accent table?"

He walked out of the back bedroom covered with sawdust and sweat, wearing a tool belt and a sheepish grin. He wore a threadbare gray T-shirt and shorts that showed off his well-muscled legs, and Sheri's mouth went dry at the sight of all that spectacular flesh on display.

"This afternoon," he replied, reminding Sheri she'd asked a question. "I wanted to do a little work around here, and this gave me something to do while I kept an eye on the boys."

She ran her hand over the table, dumbfounded. "It's beautiful. I can't believe you had time to make this. It's so much better than that garage sale thing I had sitting here."

"I still need to stain it, but it's all sanded." He grinned and reached for her hand. "My dad is a woodworker. He taught me a lot of his tricks. Come on, I'll show you the best part. The boys just went down for a nap, so they're out like a light."

He towed her toward the bedroom, and Sheri felt a surge of lust lick its way through her body. They rounded the corner and Sam pulled her inside, stopping in front of the bed. He squeezed her hand.

"What do you think?"

She blinked at the bed. "Is this your idea of foreplay?"

"Not that," he said, dipping a finger under her chin and raised her eyes from the bed to the closet. "That."

"Oh," Sheri gasped. She had shelves. And hanging racks. And a complete organization system for her shoes and belts and even a little spot for her warmer sweaters high up in a cubby near the ceiling.

"My God," she breathed, reaching out to touch the sleeve of a blouse. He'd even hung everything up when he was done building. "Martha Stewart would shit a brick. This is amazing. How did you know—"

"Last night. I noticed you'd been throwing clothes on the chair, and when I was in here making the bed this morning, I saw you had the lousiest closet storage space in history."

"This is incredible. It must've taken forever."

He shrugged and adjusted his tool belt on his hips. "It's easier than it looks. Just a few measurements and a couple trips to Home Depot for tools and materials and voilà! New closet space."

She shook her head, still in a state of disbelief. She turned to Sam, who looked sweaty and disheveled and dusty and so desirable she could barely remain standing upright.

Hey, there's an idea—

No! Get a grip, Sheri. It's just a closet.

But gratitude and surprise and lust were brewing a strong cocktail in her brain, and she was having trouble remembering her pledge not to lay a hand on him.

We already slept together once. Maybe just one more time—

No!

But maybe if we don't actually have sex—
She licked her lips, hesitating.
To hell with it.

"I feel like I should do something for you now," she said, smiling at him as she leaned across the bed to grab a pillow. She struggled a little to free it—damn hospital corners—but she pulled it to her and hugged it against her chest.

He eyed her warily. "Er, what did you have in mind?"

Sheri gave him a wicked grin and opened her arms, releasing the pillow. It fell to the ground at his feet, and she smiled wider.

"Ooops! Clumsy me. I'll just pick that up."

She sank to her knees on the pillow, running her hands over his thighs on her way down. He was wearing shorts, and she could feel every muscle in his thick thighs. She moved her palms upward until she found the buckle on the edge of the tool belt. With a quick flick of her thumb, she released it, catching the tool-laden leather before it hit the ground. She set it aside and reached for the fly on his shorts, hearing his sharp hiss of breath as he realized what she was up to.

"Sheri, I don't think we should—"

"*We* aren't doing anything. *I* am. Hush," she said, and popped open the button. She drew the zipper down quickly before he could pull away, then slid her hands into his boxer briefs.

He was already hard and ready.

"Maybe we should talk about—*oh Christ Almighty*, what are you—*holy fuck*."

Sheri stifled a laugh as she swirled her tongue around the velvety tip, teasing with light, soft strokes. She wrapped her hand around the base of him and used the other hand to shove his shorts and boxers over his hips and down to the floor. She ran her hand back up his leg, digging her nails into one firm butt cheek to hold him in place in case he tried to flee.

"Jesus," he gasped as she gripped him harder, taking more of him into her mouth. Her fingers circled him, and she angled her head to the side, testing his response, testing her own abilities.

He tasted good and she breathed him in, enjoying the faint whisper of sawdust and the thick heat of him in her mouth.

"You're driving me crazy," he said through clenched teeth.

She drew back, running her tongue across the underside of his shaft as she smiled up at him. "That's sorta the idea."

She drew him into her mouth again, taking him as deeply as she could. He was dauntingly large, but Sheri had practice. Well, sorta. She had a book Kelli bought her when she'd announced her divorce. *Tickle His Pickle* was the title, and Kelli had grinned when she'd presented it.

"Your asshole ex didn't deserve anything more erotic than a kick in the balls with steel-toed boots, but someday you'll meet a man who's worthy of a good blow job," Kelli had informed her. "You should be prepared."

I'm prepared, Sheri thought now, using suction to pull him against the roof of her mouth before releasing and letting him slide back, almost all the way out.

"Jesus," Sam hissed. He twined his fingers in her hair, but didn't put any pressure on her head. He stroked her hair, gently, politely.

Sheri didn't need polite.

She drew back and smiled up at him. "Pull my hair."

"What?"

"You heard me. Pull my hair. Move my head. Show me how you like it."

He blinked, then nodded, uttering a curse under his breath as she drew him into her mouth again, careful to cover her teeth with her lips. A shudder of pleasure coursed through her belly as she felt his hands tighten on her scalp, felt him twining her curls around his fingers.

He guided her cautiously at first, making it clear he wasn't entirely comfortable forcing himself on her—*into* her. She sucked harder.

"Sheri," he gasped, twisting his hands in her hair, driving himself deeper into her mouth.

She smiled around him and flicked her tongue in the soft groove on the underside of his shaft. She reached for the front of her blouse and undid one button, then another and another until her shirt fluttered in the breeze from the ceiling fan above. Her nipples puckered beneath her blue lace bra.

She shrugged the shirt over her shoulders and let it fall to the floor behind her. She tossed it away and rearranged herself to give him the best view.

Sam groaned and leaned down to cup her breasts in his massive palms. The movement made him sway, and he braced himself against the wall, his hands still cupping her breasts.

"Beautiful. So beautiful."

"Mmmm." Sheri could feel every contour of him as she enveloped him with her mouth. She shifted her legs, aware of her own arousal. She drew her hand down her abdomen and moved lower, feeling the seam of her panties through the thin cotton of her skirt. She pressed the heel of her hand against her pubic bone.

"Slip your hand up your skirt," Sam murmured. "Are you wearing panties?"

Sheri nodded, felt him glide against the roof of her mouth with the gesture.

"Take off your panties and touch yourself."

She pulled back and grinned. "Never say I can't take orders," she whispered, and reached up her skirt to tug off the flimsy lace thong. She tossed it into the corner. "You should take off your shirt, too."

"Yes, ma'am," he said, and pulled the gray T-shirt over his shoulders at lightning speed. She smiled at the gorgeous expanse of bare flesh, wishing she could devour every inch of him.

She'd settle for these inches, though.

She lowered her head to run her tongue over him again. She licked him like a cherry Popsicle, moving up, down, around—

"Touch yourself," he whispered. "Please."

Sheri complied, tentatively at first. She dropped her hand between her legs, parting her thighs as much as possible in a snug skirt. Her knees pressed hard into the pillow as she moved her palm up the inside of her thighs. She hesitated again, then slowly drew one finger between her slick folds.

"Oh," she gasped as Sam slid against her tongue. He gripped her hair, guiding himself toward the back of her throat. Sheri dipped her head back, letting him go deeper as she circled her own silky warmth with her fingertip.

God, she was wet.

"That feels so good," he murmured, and Sheri moaned,

wondering how the vibration felt against him. "Think of me touching you," he whispered. "Think of my hand between your legs, my fingers moving inside you."

His hands were still in her hair, while her own fingers fluttered between her legs, making her brain buzz. Sam thrust against her tongue and she felt herself inching closer to the edge.

"Sheri, I'm going to— You should stop."

She drew him deeper, plunging her fingers into herself as her thumb swirled over her swollen clit and the pressure built higher.

"Oh Christ!" Sam gasped, and she felt the first shudder of his climax in her hand, in her mouth, at the back of her throat. She swallowed, taking him in, craving more of him. He clutched her scalp as he pulsed again, and Sheri felt her whole world tilt as the heat between her legs sent her spiraling through a cloud of heat and pleasure.

She circled the pad of her thumb over her sensitive spot, her mouth tingling with the taste of him as she swallowed and writhed and cried out, plunging her fingers deep inside herself to feel the tight clench of her muscle and the endless waves of pleasure.

Her hand clutched him still, staying with him until she felt his legs start to buckle and his hands go slack in her hair. Slowly, she felt herself drift down from the clouds.

She sat back on her heels and smiled up at him, licking her lips.

"Holy God," Sam gasped, releasing her hair and stooping down to lift her up by the arms. He cradled her against his body, looking her in the eyes with a dazed expression. "That was unbelievable."

She grinned, feeling a little dazed herself. "I really liked the table. And my new closet."

He laughed, scooping her up in his arms and carrying her to the bed. He used his knee to nudge the covers back, then tucked her inside. He crawled in behind her, curling his body around hers. His right forearm rested under her head, his left forearm cradled her breasts, and everything else just fit into place as their bodies melded beneath the covers. Sam drew the sheet up over them and breathed into her hair.

"For the record, that's not why I built the table," he said. "Or the closet."

"I know. But thank you. For all of it, I mean."

He laughed and shifted his arm around her, rolling her onto her other side. They faced each other now, his blue eyes boring into hers with an intensity that made her gut clench. For a moment, they just looked at each other. The silence stretched out, and Sheri felt a prickle of anxiety.

"You have a nice singing voice," she blurted. "'The Marines' Corps Hymn'—I hadn't heard that for years. It reminded me of my grandfather. I didn't realize you had an uncle in the Marines."

He nodded once, his expression guarded. "I don't like to talk about it much."

"Oh, I'm sorry—did he—was he killed in the line of duty?"

Sam seemed to hesitate, then nodded again. "Suicide bomber."

"I'm sorry. That must have been terrible. It explains a lot, though. About you, I mean."

"How's that?"

"'The Marines' Corps Hymn,' the hospital corners on the beds—you and your uncle must have been close?"

"Yes," he said softly, brushing a strand of hair away from her face. "Were you and your grandfather close?"

"Very. He used to sing that song to me all the time, and then he'd take out his medals and let me look through them. He was such a sweet man. So gentle and kind." She swallowed, undone by this new level of intimacy between them. "I know I sound like an anti-military bitch sometimes, and it's hard not to think that way after Jonathan and my control-freak brothers and my over-the-top military parents, but—"

She trailed off, not entirely sure what she meant to say. He stroked a finger under her chin, his eyes meeting hers with understanding.

"They're not all like that," he murmured. "My uncle, your grandfather—there are good men out there. Honorable, honest, decent, respectful men."

His eyes bored into hers, and there was something there. Something she hadn't seen before. She thought he might kiss her again, that they might make love slowly this time. His expression was oddly serious, and she resisted the urge to shiver.

Sam swallowed. "We need to talk."

Chapter Fifteen

"Talk?"

Sam winced. The sound of Sheri's sweet voice echoing his suggestion back to him made him want to punch himself in the face. Hard.

The word sounded lame, even to his ears. Especially considering how abysmally he'd just failed at his plan to nip things in the bud with Sheri.

If that's what failure feels like, imagine success with this woman.

He shook his head to clear his thoughts, closing his eyes for a moment to avoid the intensity of her liquid brown eyes boring into his. He couldn't do this. He couldn't keep lying to her and then fooling around like this.

Lying is the absolute worst thing. Worse than riptides and parking tickets and pubic lice combined.

He opened his eyes again and plunged forward with his plan, despite wanting to cradle her warm body against his chest and fall asleep with her in his arms.

"Talk," he repeated, stroking a finger over her cheek. God, her skin was soft. "About this thing between us."

She gave him a funny half smile that made his gut twist. "That's just such a girly thing to suggest after sex."

Sam winced, though he had to agree. "I know. And given my career choice, I'm already aware that I may need to demonstrate my masculinity by bench-pressing your car or providing you with lab tests showing my testosterone score."

"From what I could tell five minutes ago, your testosterone is just fine."

She was smiling, but she looked wary, and Sam couldn't say he blamed her. He sighed. "I was planning to talk before sex. Actually, I wasn't planning on there being any sex. I kinda messed that part up."

"I believe we have a former president who wouldn't define it as sex, so you're good there." She cleared her throat and grazed one fingertip over his arm. He watched her play connect-the-dots with the dusting of freckles on his forearm, not meeting his eyes, and his heart ached with the urge to lie here like this forever.

"What was it you wanted to talk about?" she asked, bringing him crashing back to reality.

"We can't do this."

He watched her hold her breath for a moment, then release it slowly. "I know."

"Believe me, I love this. I loved last night and I loved everything just now. I wouldn't go back and undo it if I could. But you have to understand, I can't, in good conscience, have any sort of relationship with you."

"Because of my brother?"

"It's not just that," Sam argued, knowing it probably wouldn't make sense to her. "I made a promise to Mac, yes, but it's more than that."

"Promise." She repeated the word like it was "herpes" or "politicians."

"I made a promise," he repeated, stubbornly. "A stupid promise, I'll give you that. But it's still a promise, and I made it to my best friend. A guy who saved my life."

Sheri frowned. "Saved your life? When?"

Shit. Shit, shit, shit, he thought. God, he was bad at this lying thing.

"In college," Sam said. "The whole football team took a trip to the beach, and I got pulled out by a rogue wave. Your brother kept me from drowning."

Sheri frowned deeper, the gesture making a sweet little crease between her eyebrows that Sam longed to trace with the tip of his finger.

"And you're thinking that binds you to a lifetime of keeping your pants zipped around his sister?" she said.

He shook his head, wishing he could tell her more, but he couldn't. "I know it sounds dumb when you put it that way. But there's a code of honor—"

"Oh, for fuck's sake." She sat up, pulling the covers with her and leaving Sam's shoulders bare. "I grew up in a military family, and I married a Navy jerk. I've spent my whole life hearing about codes of honor, and it never added up to anything."

"Look, I know how strongly you feel about lying. I'd think you'd be the world's staunchest supporter of me keeping my word to Mac. Besides, I'm not the only one who thinks it would be ridiculous for us to get involved. Didn't you say the same thing yourself?"

"I know, *I know*!" She flopped onto her back and groaned. "I tell myself I'm going to be strong and self-sufficient and not fall into the same old trap of needing a man around, and then I go hopping into bed with you the first chance I get."

She threw the covers back and jumped out of bed as though the mere act would undo what they'd just done. He missed her heat instantly

"No more," she said, rummaging around on the floor for her discarded clothes. "Seriously, I mean it this time. We can't keep giving in to our urges."

Sam watched her pull on her panties and and fought the urge to peel them back off and start all over again.

"I wish it could be different," he said. "I really do."

She turned and looked at him, her face so sweet and soft and flushed and that his heart nearly split in two.

"Me, too," she said. "But this is how it has to be."

• • •

Sheri got home after dark the next day, regretful a long meeting had kept her late at the office. She hoped that wouldn't be a habit. She loved her career, and desperately wanted to do well at this job, but not if it meant leaving her boys all the time in the care of a nanny.

Not even a manny as amazing as Sam.

She felt a twinge of guilt as she thought about Jonathan's words the other night. He'd said she wasn't equipped to raise the boys alone. That she wasn't enough for them.

To hell with him.

She didn't want Jonathan back—that was for damn sure.

But was it so wrong to want a partner in parenthood?

As she shut off her headlights, she was surprised to see Sam sitting in his Jeep in the driveway. His expression said he was a million miles away, though Sheri could see he had an eye on the boys latched into their car seats in back.

She jumped out of her car and approached the Jeep from behind. His windows were down, and the light breeze ruffled his hair in the moonlight.

"Rough day?" she asked, stepping up to the Jeep.

He looked up and gave her a tired smile. "Not too bad. The boys were a little fussy, so it was kind of long."

She tried not to smile, but couldn't help it. "Is it wrong if I say I'm kinda glad?"

He quirked an eyebrow at her. "You want me to suffer?"

"No—I mean, I'm sorry it was a tough day and all, but it's nice to see you're human. That you're not some baby-soothing superhero while I spend half my time wondering if there's an off switch to make them stop crying."

He popped open the door of his Jeep. "You've seen them fussy plenty of the time with me. I took them to the store today to find stuffed peacocks. I got them these beanie ones that are a little bigger than I wanted, but it was all we could find. Jackson ended up throwing his at an old lady in the checkout line, while Jeffrey screamed so loudly the manager came over and asked us to leave."

She laughed, hoping that wasn't too rude. "Is that where you were when I came home for lunch?"

"Lunchtime?" He frowned. "No, that was probably when we were at the farmers' market. Or maybe when I took them out in the jogging stroller after nap time. Things kinda blur together on these long days."

She looked at him again, enjoying the way the moonlight made the hairs on his arms gleam golden against the curve of muscle in his arms. The soft scent of tropical flowers hung on the breeze, and the ocean air clung to her skin like a soothing net of warmth. She wished like hell she didn't want him so badly.

He turned to grab Jeffrey's car seat out of the back, and Sheri got distracted studying his ass. God, what a beautiful ass. Well-proportioned and muscular with just the right amount of—

"Would you mind grabbing Jackson?" he asked.

"Right," she said, shaking herself out of her lustful daze as she walked around to the other side of the car, muttering to herself as she went.

A normal mom *would instinctively grab her child out of the car before ogling a hot guy's backside.*

"What?" Sam called from the other side of the Jeep.

"Nothing," she replied.

"If I hear you say the phrase 'normal mom' one more time, I'm going to wash your mouth out with soap."

She laughed, though it sounded wistful even to her own ears. She pulled Jackson out of the backseat and looped the carrier over her arm, balancing her large purse on the other side. Sam strode around the Jeep and came to stand beside her, pausing to brush the hair back from her face.

"*Comparison is the thief of joy,*" he said. "Have you heard that quote before?"

"No. Who said it?"

"I'm not sure. Theodore Roosevelt, I think. Do you know why I said it just now?"

She shook her head, not sure she trusted her own voice right then.

"Because you need to stop comparing yourself to those so-called *normal moms*. You need to quit thinking there's something wrong with you if you don't respond exactly the way you think you ought to in a maternal capacity. You're your own kind of normal. And your boys love you very much."

"You sound like Dr. Spock."

Sam frowned. "From *Star Trek*?"

"From the most famous book on childrearing ever written, goofball. Isn't that like the textbook of manny training?"

"Right. Absolutely." He grabbed the baby carrier from her arm, hefting it with ease. She watched as he strode up the driveway, balancing her babies one on each side as he carried them to the porch. He set them off to the side before pulling open the screen door and digging his keys out of his pocket.

From behind, she watched his shoulders stiffen.

"The door is unlocked."

"What?"

"It's unlocked." He turned to face her, his expression stony.

"I was having trouble with it earlier, but—"

"Stay here," he commanded, pointing to the baby carriers. "Stay back from the door and keep them out of the way."

"But—"

"Don't move an inch. Stay right in that spot until I tell you otherwise."

He put his shoulder to the door and pushed as Sheri stood too stunned to protest. He charged into the house, slamming the door behind him.

She waited in the silence, alone and blinking in the darkness.

Chapter Sixteen

Sam stormed through the front door, giving a passing thought to how much easier it was to breach an entryway without having to worry about explosives. That simplified things. He started to turn the lights on, then hesitated. He'd once seen a warehouse in Sadr City wired to explode the instant someone flipped the light switch.

This is a suburban home, not a war zone.

Still, he couldn't be too careful. Not without knowing what the threat might be, and he knew there was a threat. He could feel it in his bones.

He slipped one hand under the newly built entry table, retrieving the Marine-issued .45-caliber Colt Close Quarter Battle Pistol from the secret compartment he'd built there. He grabbed the night-vision goggles he'd stashed there, too, donning them in a quick, fluid motion.

He drew the gun to his chest, gripping it with both hands as he stepped toward the sharp corner separating the living room and dining area. Adrenaline pulsed through him as he scanned the room, keeping his breathing even so his hands stayed steady.

"Who's here?" he barked. "Identify yourself *now*!"

No reply.

He kept his elbows tucked in, both hands on the weapon as he leaned his body slightly toward the interior of the room. His eyes sliced the dark space in vertical motion, moving from one end to the other with meticulous precision.

All clear.

With his lead foot on the apex of the corner, he pivoted, scanning the dining area, keeping his eyes in line with where he aimed. The gun was steady in his hands, as natural there as a glass of water or a set of car keys. He peered into the dining room, mentally cataloging every chair, every napkin.

Nothing looked out of place. He studied the bouncy chairs, the crumpled baby bib on the counter, the vase of half wilted flowers Sheri's parents had sent for her first day at work.

Sam turned again, semicircle complete. He crossed to the threshold of the kitchen, conscious of the fatal funnel, of the danger that this could be the choke point for an ambush. His shoulders were tense, but his grip on the tan metal of the pistol didn't waver. He scanned the kitchen, watching, waiting, braced for the threat.

He pivoted back toward the bedrooms, toward potential danger. He kept his back to the wall, approaching the boys' room first.

He touched the door, noting the closed position. It was open when they left, he was sure of it.

Goddammit.

Sam gripped the handle, doing a soft check to see if it was locked. It wasn't. He drew his weapon to close-contact firing position, ready to push the door open, braced to confront the intruder.

"Sam? What the hell?"

Sam spun around, stunned to see Lieutenant Limpdick standing in the doorway of the master bedroom. His hands were behind his back, holding something. Did he have a weapon? Sam trained the pistol on Limpdick's chest.

"Get your hands where I can see them—both of them—*right fucking now*!"

Limpdick's eyes fell to the firearm and went wide. He brought his hands in front of him. They held a vase of red roses.

"What the hell?" Limpdick demanded, reaching out to flip on the hall light. "Unarmed man, here."

Sam lowered his weapon, squinting at the roses in case it was a trap.

No trap. They were just flowers, nothing odd about them. He yanked off his night-vision goggles and blinked as his eyes adjusted to the sudden rush of light. Limpdick stood frozen, hands still gripping the vase.

"What the hell are you doing in here?" Sam sputtered, reorienting himself to the situation. "How did you get in? And where the hell is your car?"

Limpdick shook his head, his eyes still fixed on Sam's gun. "A cab dropped me off. I wanted to spend time with Sheri and the boys." He nodded at the pistol. "Seriously—what's going on here?"

"How the fuck did you get in? Answer me!"

"The door was unlocked. I just wanted to talk to my wife

and see my boys."

"Your *ex*-wife!" Sam snapped. "She's not your property, and neither is this house. You can't just walk in here like you own the place. If I ever catch you trespassing again, I won't even bother calling the cops. I'll blow your brains out and ask questions later."

Limpdick stared at the gun, studying it. Then he nodded once. "Understood."

Sam glanced over his shoulder, relieved to see Sheri hadn't followed. She wouldn't be aware of anything that had just transpired. He flipped the safety on the pistol and tucked it in the back of his shorts, pulling his T-shirt over it.

"I take home security and the safety of household members very seriously," Sam said.

"No shit." Limpdick frowned. "They teach you how to clear a room military-style in manny school?"

"Yes. They're very thorough."

Limpdick raised an eyebrow. "I may be a Navy man, but I know that Colt you're packing is the new standard-issue weapon of choice for the Marine Corps. They made 10,000 of them last summer for elite Special Ops troops, didn't they? Coyote brown, special release. And those night-vision goggles—those aren't the kind civilians buy at Walmart."

Sam stared him down, silent. He refused to acknowledge his cover was blown.

Limpdick shook his head. "You're a Marine, aren't you? That's what this is about. Her brothers sent you."

Sam gritted his teeth, but said nothing. "If you have a problem with me, take it up with Mac."

"I'm not interested in talking to Mac." He lowered his hands, setting the roses on the hall table. "I showed up and found the door unlocked. I wanted to make sure everything was okay, and I wanted to talk to Sheri—to get her to *listen* to me. She needs to see reason. We belong together, as a family."

Sam shook his head, grateful he'd put the pistol away so he wouldn't be tempted to shoot him. "You don't break into a woman's house to convince her you belong together. Sheri's already made up her mind."

"Where is she? I just need to talk with her."

Limpdick started toward the door, but Sam put his hand out, stopping him. "I'm asking the questions here. Why are the lights out?"

"I wanted to surprise Sheri."

"Surprise," Sam scoffed. "A romantic little ambush? Get out. Get out *now*."

Jonathan frowned. "You have no right to order me around in my own home."

"For the last time, this isn't your goddamn home!" Sam snapped. "It never has been. And Sheri isn't your wife. I'm going to go out and ask her if she wants me to call the police, or if she'd like to let you see the boys one last time before you leave. Either way, I'm watching every fucking move you make, and then I'm going to drive your ass to the airport and make sure you get on your goddamn plane."

"My flight isn't for more than a week."

"You're trying my last shred of patience here," Sam barked. "Be grateful you don't have a bullet between your eyes."

Sam turned and stalked back to the doorway, pausing to tuck the Colt and the night-vision goggles back in the secret compartment. He pushed the front door open, surprised to see Sheri still standing exactly where he'd left her.

"You obeyed my order," he said.

"Don't sound so surprised." She smiled up at him, and Sam felt his heart twist. "I figure if one of us is going to get shot confronting an intruder, it should be you. I don't want to leave the boys motherless."

"Smart woman." Sam took a deep breath. "Jonathan is here."

"What? How on earth did he get in?"

"He claims the door was unlocked."

She opened her mouth to say something, then frowned. "That might be right. I came home for lunch when I found out I'd be working late tonight. I was having trouble with the lock, and I was in a hurry and—dammit, this is my fault."

"No," Sam insisted. "It's not your fault. A man can't just walk into your house, not even if the door is unlocked. It's trespassing."

She hugged her arms around her elbows. "I'm sorry, Sam. I'll be more careful."

"It's okay. Want me to call the police?"

She hesitated. "Let me talk to him first. He wants to see the boys?"

"He wants to see you, too."

Sheri glanced down at the babies, who were fast asleep in their carriers. "Can you watch them for a second? I'd like to give him a piece of my mind before he gets distracted pretending to play daddy."

He shook his head. "I'm not leaving you alone with him. Not after what he pulled tonight."

"You can stay within earshot. Please? I just need a second."

He hesitated, then bent down and picked up the infant

carriers. "I'm following you inside, and I'll give you some space. But if he so much as lays a finger on you—"

"Thank you, Sam. Truly."

Sheri walked through the door, her stride purposeful and confident, even though Sam could see her hands were shaking. She marched right up to her ex-husband and folded her arms over her chest.

"Never again, do you hear me? You do not *ever*, under any circumstances, enter my home without my express permission."

"You're being unreasonable, Sheridan. I just wanted to talk with you, and I haven't been able to get you to listen. We just need to sit down together and—"

"No! Let's get one thing clear here. We are not sitting down together, nor are we standing up, lying down, or assuming any position together besides that of two people who happen to share a whole lot of animosity and two really amazing kids. Do I make myself clear?"

"We're a family, Sheridan."

Limpdick started to reach for her, and Sam braced himself to pounce. She beat him to it, smacking Limpdick's hand away as she took a step back.

"We belong together," Jonathan tried again.

Sam set the baby carriers at the edge of the living room, out of Limpdick's line of sight. He checked to be sure the boys were still sleeping, then positioned himself in the corner of the room. He stood at ease, thumbs interlaced behind his back.

"You gave up your rights to me and to this family when you walked out on us," Sheri said. "When you betrayed me."

Sam tried not to wince as he thought about betrayal. Was he really much better than Jonathan?

"You slept with a stripper, for chrissakes," Sheri snapped. "In our goddamn marriage bed while I was taking the boys to the doctor for a checkup."

Okay, maybe he was a little better than Jonathan.

"Surely you're aware that wasn't all my fault," Jonathan replied. "What was I supposed to do? We hadn't been intimate for weeks, and a man has certain needs."

"You're insane!" Sheri yelled. "I gave birth to twins— your children, might I remind you. You'll have to forgive me if I didn't hop straight off the delivery table to ride the baloney pony."

"There's no need to be rude, Sheridan."

"Actually, I think this is exactly the sort of situation that requires it." She took a deep breath and a step back. "Look, I'm not going to have this conversation with you. Say what you need to say to the boys, and then I'd like you to leave. If you pull anything like this again, I'm reporting you to your command."

Jonathan scowled at her, then shot a hateful look at Sam. "Like she's any good in the sack, anyway. Take my advice, man—don't bother with this one. She makes cold fish look like good bedmates. Seriously—"

It was the last word he uttered before Sam punched him squarely in the jaw.

• • •

Sheri fell into bed early that night, feeling exhausted but restless, craving Sam's touch. She slept in unfulfilling bursts and woke at the crack of dawn with no hope of drifting back into a slumber.

So much for sleeping late on a Saturday.

She rubbed her cheek against her pillowcase, certain she still smelled a faint hint of sawdust where Sam had rested his head.

Christ, was that only two days ago? Amazing how quickly things changed.

She had to admit, watching him punch Jonathan while defending her honor had been pretty hot. She may have sworn off military men, but that didn't mean she was immune to the charms of a hot, burly beefcake with an overcharged sense of responsibility, too much provider instinct, and a mean right hook.

She rolled over again, restless. A wild rooster crowed outside her window as the sun bathed the room in pale light. She could smell the sea air and a hint of something in the sheets that must've been the scent of Sam's shampoo.

She wanted to keep fighting her attraction to him, but she wasn't sure she had it in her. Seeing Jonathan and Sam together, it was clear they had nothing in common. If she was worried about Sam lying and cheating and treating her the way Jonathan had, she felt fairly certain she didn't have to fear that.

Still, there was something about Sam she couldn't quite read. Something that didn't add up. She couldn't put her finger on it, but she sensed he had secrets.

The thought of Sam and secrets sent her mind wandering down another path entirely. Did he crave her touch the way she craved his? Did he lie in bed thinking about her, wanting to wander down the hall and crawl in bed beside her?

She glanced at the clock. It wasn't even six in the morning. Was he awake yet? He was an early riser, so it was possible.

Maybe now would be a good time to discuss things. To talk about this crazy attraction between them.

Talking isn't what you have in mind, her subconscious scolded, but she was already out of bed and cinching her robe at her waist.

She padded quietly down the hall, not wanting to wake Sam or the boys. She peeked into the babies' room and saw them both curled in their cribs sleeping soundly. She paused a moment to watch them breathing, then crossed the hall to his room.

The door was open, and she hesitated, not wanting to invade his privacy. But maybe he was up, too. Maybe she could offer him some coffee or toast or—

Coffee and toast is not what you want to offer him.

She cinched her robe tighter and stepped into the doorway.

It took her a moment to register what she was seeing. Sam was seated in his desk chair facing away from her. The back of the chair covered most of his torso, but she could tell he was shirtless. Early sunlight bathed his shoulders in a warm glow.

His right arm moved rhythmically, stroking something in his lap. She could see his forearm disappearing and reappearing at the edge of the chair, moving in a steady tempo. A flash of terry cloth poking out at the edge of the chair told her he had a towel on his lap. His shoulders moved with each stroke, and she shivered with intrigue at the knowledge of what he was doing.

She knew she should leave, and give him some privacy, but she felt frozen in place. Was he thinking about her as he touched himself? What if she tiptoed in and offered to assist? What if she dropped to her knees in front of him and—

Sam whirled around. The towel in his lap masked the evidence of his arousal, but it was his expression that made Sheri take a step back.

Absolute, total horror.

He blinked at her, his face shifting from horror to guilt. "I can explain."

"Sam, I'm not—"

"Just give me a second to—"

"It's okay, I have brothers. I understand."

"No, I swear, your brothers didn't—"

"Sam, stop." She stepped forward, trying not to look at the bulge beneath the towel he'd thrown over his lap. "It's okay. We all have needs. I mean, God knows I've been working my personal massager overtime, and—"

She stopped, trying to read him. He hadn't said a word, but the bulge under the towel wasn't going away.

"Look, Sam. This is silly."

"It is?"

"I want you. You want me. It's stupid for me to be next door fantasizing about you and touching myself while you're in here like this. We should be touching each other. This is ridiculous."

She took another step forward, close enough to feel the heat of his skin. She wasn't sure if it was lust or insanity making her bold, but she didn't care. She was done dancing around this. She moved her hand to the sash on the front of her robe and untied it, shrugging the purple satin off her shoulders. She shivered as the purple satin fell to her feet, and she stood there naked before him, daring herself not to flinch.

Daring Sam not to run.

Chapter Seventeen

"My God," Sam said, closing his eyes.

It was partly the thrill of seeing her naked before him, eager and willing and so goddamn beautiful.

But it was also relief.

He couldn't believe how close he'd come to being caught. To having this whole thing blow up in his face.

He hadn't been jerking off—hell, he wouldn't have cared about that. He'd been cleaning his pistol, polishing and rubbing it down with an oilcloth the way he'd been taught to do when he was still a young Marine.

Now he just needed to get rid of the evidence.

Sam opened his eyes and looked at her, eager to lunge out of his chair and put his hands all over her. God, she was beautiful. And so very, very naked.

"Could you do me a favor?" he asked.

She nodded. "Anything you want."

"Don't ask me why. I just need you to turn around and close your eyes for ten seconds."

She looked at him curiously, then nodded. "Sure thing," she said, pivoting on her heels. "One. Two. Three—"

He picked up the towel he'd spread over his lap, gathering the cleaning rod and brushes and the parts of the pistol still disassembled. He yanked open his desk drawer and shoved the whole thing inside. He'd have to finish cleaning up later, but for now—

He stood up, reaching for her before he'd even cleared the distance between them. His hand closed around her hip, pulling her to him.

"You can turn back around."

She smiled up at him, turning with a glance toward the desk. "Nicely done," she said. "Your cleanup skills are impeccable."

"That's what I'm paid for. Sorta."

He moved his hand over her hip and across the curve of her ass, reveling in the feel of all that warm flesh beneath his palm. God, he wanted her.

"Um, look," she said, biting her lip. "I don't know how far you'd gotten when I walked in, and if you need a little time to recharge your batteries, I totally understand and we can just snuggle or—"

"Sheri?"

"Yes?"

"Shut up," he said, and lowered his mouth to hers. He kissed her softly at first, then with a fierceness that surprised even him. He pressed his body against hers, making sure she felt the evidence he was more than ready to please her.

"No recharging necessary," she breathed as he kissed his

way down her throat. "Thank God."

He devoured her everywhere at once, nipping, licking, teasing as he made his way down the center of her body. He drew one nipple into his mouth, sucking gently as his hands circled her waist. She gasped and twined her fingers in his hair. Sam moved to the other breast, licking, brushing her nipple with his stubbled cheek.

Sheri whimpered, and he felt her knees start to buckle. He caught her around the waist and held her upright.

"What do you say we try this in a bed for once," he murmured. "Just for variety."

"I thought you'd never ask."

"I'm not asking now," he said, scooping her into his arms. "I'm telling you I'm going to make love to you until neither of us can stand, so we might as well start out in a reclined position."

He tossed her onto the immaculately made queen bed, not bothering to pull the covers back. She scrambled for a moment, and he could tell she was trying to arrange herself in a flattering position, adjusting her breasts and sucking in her stomach. He caught her hands in his and shook his head.

"You're perfect exactly the way you are. It wouldn't matter if you stood on your head with your ankles at your ears and your hair on fire—you'd look amazing no matter what."

She smiled. "I'm glad you think so, because I'm pretty sure I haven't been able to pull off that ankle-to-ear thing since college."

She reached for the drawstring at the waist of his shorts and gave it a tug. He stroked her breast with one hand as she maneuvered his shorts down over his hips, her hands deft and eager and so goddamn soft.

"I want you," he said, holding her eyes with his as he knelt on the edge of the bed. "I hope you know that. I'm not just giving in because you showed up here and took your robe off. I'm doing this because I desperately, urgently want you, and if I had to wait one more minute, my brain was going to explode all over this room."

"Brains are difficult to scrub off apricot-colored walls," Sheri breathed as he bent to kiss her again. "It's a good thing I have a manny with a knack for deep cleaning."

"Lucky you."

She giggled and edged back on the bed, making room for him to lie down with her. Sam reached around her, his arms on either side of her body as he lowered himself onto her. He pinned her beneath him, reveling in the feel of her moving under him. Every part of his body touched some part of hers, from toes to knees to belly to chest.

He breathed her in, savoring the soft, floral scent of her, watching his breath rustle the wild curls framing her face.

"So beautiful. Do you have any idea how beautiful you are?"

She smiled up at him. "No. Why don't you tell me? I think I'd enjoy that."

He held her eyes with his as something clenched in his chest. "You're seriously the most amazing woman I've ever seen. I love every single part of your body. I love your hair and your breasts and your hips and your hands and that little birthmark on your shin that looks like a jellybean. Every part of you is perfect."

"I—thank you."

He pushed one of his knees between hers, forcing them

apart. His body fell naturally into the space between her legs, and she moaned beneath him.

"Yes," she whispered, arching beneath him. "Please, Sam. Don't stop."

"I don't plan to."

She gasped as he slid inside her. "I can take orders, too," he murmured.

"Thank God."

He drove into her hard, and her eyes went wide with surprise and pleasure. She gasped, arching up to meet his thrust. He moved into her again, drawing back slowly before plunging in again. Her hips rose to meet him, a rhythm that made his whole body hum with pleasure. He drew back and hesitated, her breath warm on his throat. She twined her fingers around his back, urging him on.

"What?" she gasped.

"Just slowing down," he whispered, kissing the base of her throat. "Making it last."

He moved his hips, angling his pubic bone against her to hit that perfect spot. She cried out, writhing beneath him. He drew back again, pausing there before sliding inside her, feeling her warmth sheathe every throbbing inch of him.

Her hips picked up a rhythm all their own, and he moved to match her. She quivered beneath him, crying out softly. He drew himself into her, no longer certain where her body ended and hers began.

"Please," she whispered.

He wasn't sure what she was pleading for, but he wanted it, too.

He moved again, grinding against her with exquisite slowness. His eyes locked on hers, unblinking. She gazed back, her lashes fluttering as he stroked into her. She gasped as he withdrew, pulling out of her almost completely, hesitating there at her entrance. Then he slid in again, moving with agonizing, languid strokes.

She closed her eyes and seemed to disappear into the sensation. Sam could feel himself starting to lose it, but he gritted his teeth and held on. He wanted this to last forever.

She cried out, rocking her hips beneath him as she pressed her body tightly against his. Her breath was warm in his ear, and he smelled jasmine in her hair. She bit his shoulder as he glided out, then in again.

"Yes," she breathed, arching tight against him. "*Yes*."

She dug her nails into his shoulder blades as Sam drove into her again. He was still moving slowly, but his brain was swirling fast now. His breath came quick and hot, with hers matching the fevered pace.

She circled her hips, grinding her body against his. Sam groaned, whispered her name, drove himself deeper. She was close. He could feel it. Her fingers clenched around his shoulders as she gasped, riding the first wave as it began to crest. He thrust into her and gave a low moan in the back of his throat.

"Ohmygod!" she whimpered.

Sam thrust into her again, tipping her over the edge. She cried out, digging her nails into his back to spur him on. He thrust into her, his breath coming in fevered gasps until he felt something inside him break loose. Spots of color exploded behind his eyes as she clenched her thighs around him.

Everything burst into a million bits of bliss as he drove into her again and again and again.

They lay there panting afterward, their bodies glued together as the ceiling fan whirred overhead.

"My God," she breathed, turning her head to look at him. He was still half on top of her, not sure he'd ever be able to move again.

He smiled her. "My thoughts exactly."

Sheri laughed and wriggled beneath him. Sam rolled off her, moving to his side and pulling her to his chest. She turned in his arms and smiled up at him, stroking his cheek with her palm. He drew her closer.

"You're incredible," he murmured.

"You're not so bad yourself."

"We should do that again sometime," he said.

"Seriously?"

"What, you're bored already?" He grinned, propping himself up on one elbow. "I'm tired of fighting it, Sheri. I'm nuts about you. You're nuts about me. We fit together in more ways than just this. Your brothers are going to have to deal with this sooner or later, and I vote for sooner."

She blinked, looking stunned by his words. Truth be told, Sam felt a little stunned by them himself.

"That's my vote, too," she whispered.

"You don't know how long I've wanted this," he murmured against her hair.

"Me, too. From the first day you showed up here, I've been thinking about it."

He laughed. "I have you beat by miles, babe. The first time I saw you—back when you were this sassy, wild-haired sister of one of my friends. I wanted you the first moment I laid eyes on you. I never stopped wanting you. Not just like this, but all the time. I want you when you're laughing and when you're crying and when you're blowing up blenders or singing off-key in the shower. I want you all the time, no matter what."

She swallowed, completely undone by his words. "I don't know what to say."

"Say you'll give me a chance. Give us a chance, to hell with your brothers."

"I'm in." She grinned and planted a kiss on his lips. He returned the kiss, then drew back, pulling her tighter against him.

"Good," he said, closing his eyes again. "What do you want to do today?"

"How about the beach?"

"Perfect. But how about we enjoy this for just a little bit longer?"

"Deal."

She snuggled against him, and every molecule of Sam's body swelled with pleasure as he held her close and breathed her in. He stroked his hand over the curve of her hip, certain he'd never felt anything so soft. Certain he could lie like this forever.

Certain he was falling in love with her.

• • •

Sheri woke alone in Sam's bed with the smell of bacon hanging in the air. She located her robe on the floor and padded into the dining area to find him cooking breakfast. Before she could insist on making her own food, Sam handed her a plate of bacon and eggs and pointed to a chair.

"Sit. Eat."

She opened her mouth to argue, then decided against it. "Thank you."

"You're welcome."

She dropped into the chair and picked up a fork. "You know, you don't have to feed me on weekends. Or any day of the week, really, but especially not weekends. You should take days off."

"I have to eat anyway," he said. "Besides, I told Mac I'd take care of you. This is taking care of you."

She studied his back, broad and muscular, and shivered with the memory of what that back had felt like beneath her palms only an hour ago. She smiled as she watched him butter a piece of toast at the counter. He turned and handed it to her before sitting down on the opposite end of the table.

"You've been talking to Mac a lot lately?" she asked.

He hesitated, then bit into a piece of toast. "On occasion."

"Is he checking up on me? Requiring you to give him up-to-the-minute reports?"

She hated the petulance in her own voice, but she also hated the idea of her brothers spying on her. Sam regarded her warily.

"No." He bit into his toast again. "Any new phone calls or text messages from Jonathan?"

She shrugged and reached over to tickle Jackson in his high chair. The baby giggled and waved an arm, smacking himself in the face. Jeffrey wailed for a few seconds before dissolving into giggles.

"I had a text message from Jonathan in the middle of the night," she said. "He wants to talk to me about you. I ignored it."

"About me?" Sam frowned. "Did he say why?"

She shook her head. "I wouldn't worry he's going to press charges or anything. Even if you punched him, he's the one who broke into the house."

"Right." Sam frowned again and looked down at his toast. "I've got someone coming by first thing Monday to install new locks. You were right about something being wrong with the one on the front door. Until Jonathan leaves Hawaii, I'll be sleeping in the living room to keep a closer eye on it."

"Okay." She thought about his long, solid body laid out on the sofa, a sliver of moonlight falling over the thin sheet covering him. She ached to pull the sheet back and crawl in beside him.

Stop it, Sheri.

"Still want to go to the beach today?" she asked.

"Of course."

"Good. I'll get our things together. Meet you at the car in thirty minutes?"

An hour later—hampered only slightly by a twin-powered baby meltdown—they were on their way to the beach. The boys slurped on their fingers in the backseat, while Sheri hunted around for her sunglasses.

"They've both got bottom teeth coming in," he said as he turned the car off the main road. "They're starting to look like jack-o'-lanterns."

"This is where I confess that I'm glad the breastfeeding thing didn't work out for me. I wasn't looking forward to losing a nipple to baby teeth."

"Why didn't it work out?"

She glanced at him, surprised he'd asked the question. Sam took in her startled expression, then shrugged. "Sorry. I was just curious, but if you'd rather not—"

"No, it's okay. All the mothering magazines make it sound so easy. The most natural thing in the world, and so healthy for the baby. But for some women, it just doesn't work right."

She saw Sam dart a glance at her chest and she couldn't stop herself from giving a self-conscious laugh. "I know, I have all the necessary equipment. But I didn't produce enough milk, and the boys just screamed and turned red and refused to latch on. My lactation coach finally suggested—"

"Lactation coach?"

"I know, it sounds weird."

"Does she make your breasts do calisthenics?"

Sheri laughed. "No. And she finally agreed that it just doesn't work for some women. I guess that's me."

She shrugged and looked out the window, feeling stupidly self-conscious.

"Is that why you're always making those comments about not being a normal mom?"

"One of dozens of reasons, really. I love the boys to death. Sometimes I just don't know that I got the right wiring, that's all. Then when Jonathan shows up and starts making noise about how I'm not enough for them as a single mom..."

She shrugged, trailing off. Sam shook his head as he turned onto the small side road leading to PMRF. She started to point him toward the correct branch of a fork in the road, but he took it without needing her guidance.

"That's bullshit," Sam said. "Don't let Jonathan's crap get to you. You're an amazing mom. Just one of you is worth a dozen of your so-called *normal moms*." He rolled down his window as they approached the entry gate. "Did you ever think that's the thing that'll make you a really excellent mother in the long run?"

"What?"

"The fact that you aren't some absurd Stepford wife of a mother who follows the imaginary rule book to a tee," he said. "The fact that you're not afraid to play in the mud or tell crude jokes or catch bugs. The fact that you can be firm and maternal, but you're fun, too. That's something the boys are going to appreciate when they're older." He hesitated, glancing away as they approached the entry gate. Then he looked at her again, his blue eyes boring into her. "It's what I appreciate about you."

Sheri swallowed hard, her throat suddenly tight with emotion. "Sam, I—"

"Morning, sir. Oh, hello."

The gate guard approached the car and shook Sam's hand like they were old friends. Then he nodded at Sheri. "Ma'am, good to see you again."

Sheri leaned across Sam's lap and handed over her paperwork. "Morning, Thomas. We're just here to spend the day at the beach."

"Of course, Ms. Patton-Price. You know the way?"

"I already have my favorite spot on the beach."

The man nodded and shuffled through the paperwork. "Okay then. Looks like everything's in order. I'll see you when you stop back by on your way out. Have a great day."

"You too, Thomas."

"Sir," he said, nodding at Sam.

Sam adjusted his dark glasses and nodded back. "Mahalo."

They drove through the gate and continued down the

road. Sheri pointed out a few buildings, showing Sam where the family housing areas and skateboard park were as they made their way toward her favorite beach spot.

"You like it here, then," he said, angling the car into a parking spot.

"Very much."

"Good. It's good to have a job you love."

"Do you love your job?"

Sam grinned and stepped out of the car, stooping down to scoop up Jackson while Sheri bustled around to the other side and unlatched Jeffrey's carrier from the car seat base.

She looked up to see him watching her with a smile that made her toes curl against her flip-flops. "I love my job more than you could possibly imagine."

Chapter Eighteen

Once they found their spot on the beach, Sam made three trips back to the car to shuttle towels and coolers and enough baby gear to care for three dozen infants. Finally, he sat back in a beach chair to watch the boys fling sand around with the little green shovels. He was ready to grab them away if either baby looked ready to spoon up a mouthful of it.

"Would you mind if I went for a quick dip in the ocean?" Sheri asked.

He turned to look at her and felt a stir of arousal that was growing all too familiar. "Will that require you stripping down to just a bikini?"

She grinned. "If I say yes, are you going to ogle me as I walk to the water?"

"I'm going to ogle you no matter what."

"I plan to hold you to that."

"It won't be hard. Speaking of hard things—"

She swatted him with a towel and stood up. "We were

not speaking of hard things. By the way, did I tell you Mac's coming to visit again soon?"

"He is?"

Christ, Sam thought. *He'll take one look at us and know in an instant we've slept together.*

"I know what you said this morning about putting it all out there for my brothers, but if you're not ready—" She bit her lip. "Well, I'm not totally sure I'm ready."

"No, it's great," Sam said, ignoring the dread pooling in his chest. "Can't wait to see him again. Speaking of things I haven't seen for a while, why are you still wearing a shirt?"

Sheri laughed and pulled off her top. She wore a bright-red bikini top in sports bra style. More conservative than those stringy styles Sam saw everywhere in Hawaii, but somehow even hotter on Sheri.

"You're beautiful," he said without thinking.

"Thank you." She smiled and stood up. "If all you can do is grope me with your eyes at the moment, then I guess I'd better make it worth your while."

She shucked her cotton shorts and stood there for a moment with her curves silhouetted against the sun. Her hair was loose and wild, and the low-rise red bikini bottoms showed off her fabulous ass in a way that made Sam grateful he'd opted for loose-fitting swim trunks. "That's worth every second of the excruciating agony my testicles will be experiencing for the next few hours."

Sheri laughed and tossed her hair. "You're such a romantic." She turned and jogged off down the beach toward the water.

He watched her go, feeling an ache that was nowhere near his balls.

When she was out of sight, he glanced down at her beach bag. He'd seen her slip her phone into the front pocket, so he shoved his hand into it, fishing around for the glittery pink case. He pulled the phone out, glancing back toward the beach to see if she was watching him.

All clear.

Sam hit the power button and saw the new message alert from Jonathan.

Must talk to you. Don't you want to know who Sam really is?

He frowned and looked back down the beach. She was waist-deep in the ocean, laughing as a soft wave splashed up and hit her in the belly. She turned and smiled at him, waving as the wind tousled her curls.

He waved back, doing his best to hide the phone in his lap.

The instant she turned around, he deleted the message.

• • •

They stayed at the beach all day, stopping to snack when they got hungry and taking turns watching the boys while the other napped or bodysurfed or explored the beach. It was an easy sort of partnership that made Sam ache to savor it for more than just a couple weeks.

The sun was beginning to drop low in the sky as they packed up their gear.

"I had a really nice time today," she said. "Thanks for being part of it."

"My pleasure. I had a great day, too. Toss me that towel

over there and I'll make the first run to the car."

He'd just stood up with both arms full of gear when an older gentleman approached from the side. He tipped his red-and-white-striped derby hat at Sheri as he slung a fishing pole over one shoulder.

"Afternoon, ma'am," he said to Sheri. "Nice to see you out here when you're not too dressed up to enjoy the weather."

She smiled back, warm and friendly, as a jolt of dread knifed through Sam's gut. Wasn't this the guy he'd met during his spy mission to PMRF a week ago? Sam pulled his baseball cap lower, trying his damnedest not to be noticed. Would the old guy remember him? They'd only spoken a few words, but Sam had admitted he was a Marine. That he was here doing a favor for a buddy.

He slid his sunglasses on and prayed the guy wouldn't remember any of it.

"I just started working at PMRF on Monday," Sheri was saying, "so it was fun to bring the whole family out here to enjoy the area. How's the fishing today?"

"Can't complain. Can I give you folks a hand?"

He turned to Sam, reaching out to take one of the beach bags. Sam watched as recognition lit up the old guy's face.

"Hey there, I almost didn't recognize you," he said, sticking out a hand for Sam to shake. "Didn't get a chance to introduce myself properly last weekend. The name's Arthur Ziegler. Retired Marine sergeant, living here now with my son and his wife and their boys."

Sam returned the handshake, glancing at Sheri to see a bewildered look on her face. "Um, pleasure to meet you, sir. I'm just going to run these things up to the car and—"

"I didn't catch your name, son." He smiled at Sheri. "Any

of your names, actually."

"I'm so sorry, this is Sam and Jackson and Jeffrey and I'm Sheri," she said. "Did you say you'd met Sam before?"

"No!" Sam said a little too quickly. "Just now. We're just now meeting, that is."

Arthur turned and gave him a curious look. "That so? Maybe I'm confusing you with someone else." He studied Sam a moment, his expression perplexed. "My memory's not what it used to be, but I coulda sworn I met you out here last weekend. You're a Marine here doing a favor for a buddy, right? I swear—"

"Nope, you must be thinking of someone else," Sam interrupted before Arthur could describe Sam's tattoo or repeat their conversation or give any further proof Sam had been here scoping out Sheri's workplace.

His face felt hot and his hands were clammy and he was pretty sure he was going to lose it completely if he didn't escape. He had to get Arthur away from Sheri. "I sure do appreciate your offer to help though, sir. Would you mind grabbing that cooler right there? The car's just up here a bit."

He started walking fast, hoping to God the old man would follow, that he hadn't already done too much damage, that his whole world wasn't about to come crashing down around him.

"Sure thing, son," Arthur said as he picked up the cooler. He fell into step beside Sam, and Sam heaved a silent sigh of relief. When they'd gone about ten paces, he turned back to look at Sheri.

She was staring after them with an odd look on her face and her phone gripped in one hand.

She wasn't smiling.

Chapter Nineteen

A sour sense of uneasiness settled into Sheri's gut and wasn't budging. She hardly spoke to Sam the whole drive home, barely noticing his efforts to draw her out and engage her in conversation about what she wanted for dinner and when she thought the boys might start crawling.

Why had Arthur Ziegler been so sure he recognized Sam? The guard at the gate had seemed pretty friendly, too. Had Sam been to PMRF to check on her?

Or was there something more going on here?

It was the *something more* that niggled at Sheri all evening. She made a simple dinner of pork and beans and pineapple with cut-up hot dogs—another staple of her childhood—but she barely touched it.

"You okay?" Sam asked

She looked up to see him studying her warily. "I'm fine."

"Is there something you want to talk about?"

"Is there something *you* want to talk about?"

They sat frozen in an awkward stalemate. She wondered how long it might have dragged on if it weren't for Jeffrey squawking in the other room. Sheri hustled off to tend him, doling out bottles and kisses and all the motherly love she could muster.

By the time she returned to the kitchen, Sam had cleared the table. He looked up as she entered the room, a guarded look on his face.

"Have you heard from Jonathan again?" he asked.

She shook her head. "No, but I left my phone in the other room." She began loading dishes into the dishwasher, wondering what questions she should be asking. Did she really want to give a voice to her suspicions? Would that just make them real?

It was possible she was being paranoid. Jonathan's betrayal had done a number on her, after all.

She bit her lip. "Actually, I think I'm going to go find my phone. I want to call Mac."

"What for?"

She looked at him, trying to decide if he looked guilty or merely curious. "I just have some questions to ask," she said. "I think I'll turn in after that. I didn't sleep much last night."

They locked eyes, and she felt her cheeks warm up. Was he recalling what they'd been doing instead of sleeping in his bed early that morning?

"Okay." Sam nodded. "I'll finish up here. Thanks for the great day at the beach."

She smiled in spite of her grim mood, allowing him to pull her into an embrace. When his lips found hers, she dissolved into him, almost forgetting her questions, almost forgetting her suspicions, almost forgetting herself—

Almost.

"Good night, Sam," she said as she drew back.

She felt his gaze follow her down the hall and it took every ounce of strength she had not to sprint back to the kitchen and throw herself into his arms. She closed the bedroom door behind her and picked the phone up off her dresser.

No new messages, which was a relief.

She crawled into bed with all her clothes on, feeling chilled. She gripped the phone and hesitated, finger poised over the speed-dial button for Mac. Maybe she wasn't ready to confront Sam, but she could get some information from her brother. Of course, she had no idea where he was at the moment, which was nothing new. It could be the middle of the night in some war-torn country with Mac conducting whatever secret government business kept him occupied.

The hell with it. If Mac was crouched on a battlefield or boardroom somewhere, he just wouldn't answer the damn phone.

He picked up on the second ring, startling Sheri with the quick bark of his voice. "Sheri, what's up? What's wrong? Where are you?"

She burrowed into her pillow, soothed by her brother's low rumble, even if he was being an idiot. "Nice to talk to you, too, dumbass. I'm fine. For crying out loud, can't I call my brother without there being some crisis?"

"How's Sam?" Mac asked, ignoring her question. "Treating you and the boys okay?"

"Sure, Sam's great. Actually, that's what I wanted to talk to you about."

"Oh?" Mac's tone was guarded, though that didn't mean

much. Mac's tone was always guarded.

"What can you tell me about Sam?"

"What do you mean?"

"I mean that I'm getting the sense that there's more to Sam than just a happy-go-lucky manny who used to be your football teammate."

"Well, that's true," Mac said, drawing the words out slowly. "He's also an excellent harmonica player."

"Goddammit, Mac. That's not what I meant and you know it."

"I have no idea what you meant, Sheri. Sam is a top-notch manny who's great with kids and extremely competent with domestic tasks. I'd trust him with my life."

"Oh yeah?" She licked her lips, not sure what she wanted to ask next. "Have you ever had to do that?"

"Do what?"

"Trust Sam with your life?"

"He drove me to the hospital once when I got food poisoning. Then there was the time he helped pull me out of a bar fight in college."

If Mac had been standing beside her, she would have slugged him in the shoulder. Instead, she tried another tack. "Sam sure seems to have a lot of military knowledge for a civilian."

"He majored in political science. Had to take all kinds of classes in military history, plus his aunt was an officer in the Coast Guard."

"Is this aunt married to the uncle who's the Marine?"

"Uh—no. Different branch of the family. Look, Sheri. Sam's a great guy. He's one of my oldest buddies, and a stand-up character."

Sheri balled her hands into fists. This was getting her nowhere. "If Sam's so great, why did you tell him not to touch me?"

"Sam touched you?!"

Sheri pulled the phone from her ear, certain Mac's yelling could be heard on the other end of the house. She put it back in a hurry, eager to do damage control. "That's not what I said. I just wanted to know if you issued some sort of stupid order like that."

"Why would I do that?"

"You tell me."

They were both silent a moment, a sibling standoff that was all too familiar to both of them. At last, Mac cleared his throat. "When does Jonathan leave?"

"Less than a week."

"You've heard from him?"

Sheri couldn't tell if it was a question or a statement. That was true of nearly every phrase Mac uttered, and it drove her as crazy now as it had when Mac still pulled her pigtails.

"Yes, I've heard from him."

"And you're going to get better about making sure the door is locked?"

"Dammit!" she snapped, unsure whether to be irritated with Sam or with Mac. She settled for both. "You *have* been talking to Sam."

"Of course I've been talking to Sam. He's my employee, Sheri, and I have a right to know if my sister is in danger."

"I'm not in danger," she muttered.

"Well I'm going to make sure Sam keeps it that way. Is he doing an adequate job looking after you and the boys?"

"Yes," she admitted a bit grudgingly. "More than adequate."

"Are you letting him help you, or are you being difficult?"

She rolled her eyes, not sure how the conversation had gone from her interrogating Mac to Mac interrogating her. It wasn't the first time.

"I'm letting him help me," Sheri said. "Most of the time, anyway. You know, it wouldn't be wise for me to become too reliant on a man—any man—at this point in my life."

"Sheri, there is zero risk of you ever becoming too reliant on anyone because you're too stubborn."

Mac's voice had risen so it was practically a yell, and she felt herself scrunch down a little under the covers.

"Has anyone ever told you you're the biggest control freak on the planet?" she asked.

"Why do you think I'm not married?"

Sheri smiled, loving her idiot brother in spite of the fact that he was—well, an idiot. "Good night, Mac."

"Good night, Sheri. Keep your hands off Sam. And let him take care of you."

She hung up the phone and stared at it a moment. "I can't do both, you big jerk."

• • •

Sam stayed up late that night. He'd hoped Sheri might emerge from her room and tell him about her phone call, but she'd stayed behind closed doors all night. He wished he knew what she'd asked Mac. What Mac had told her in return.

All he knew is that there was a definite chill in the air, and that he was sleeping alone tonight.

Or not sleeping, as the case may be.

You've had too many close calls lately, he chided himself. *You're on the brink of screwing this whole thing up royally. Of her finding out you're a lying jerk, just like her ex.*

He honestly wasn't sure which close call bothered him the most. His freak-out over the beets? Limpdick pegging him as a military man? Two different guys recognizing him at PMRF today?

Or the fact that he'd very nearly lunged across the table over dinner, so desperate to have Sheri again that he was willing to give up his job, his honor—not to mention his home-cooked dinner—just to have her warm and lush and laughing beneath him on the dining room table?

He'd settle for a bed. Hell, he'd settle for anyplace at all she named, if he could just touch her again.

Focus, he ordered himself as he looked down at the Colt .45 in his lap. Her intrusion that morning hadn't given him a chance to finish cleaning it—not that he was complaining—but he needed to get the job done. He'd even pushed the door shut to afford himself some privacy, though he'd cracked it again when he realized he couldn't see the front door.

He'd been planning to sleep in the living room to keep watch there, but he'd already checked the lock three dozen times. There'd been no signs of Jonathan, and the lock seemed to be holding.

He wondered if he could get his hands on Sheri's phone again. Maybe he could figure out how to block messages from Jonathan's number.

That's a short-term solution, idiot. What do you plan to do long-term? You can't go on like this forever.

He couldn't think about that now.

He fired up his laptop as he ran an oilcloth over his weapon, determined to do a bit of multitasking for the evening. An alert popped up on screen from Mac.

I'm e-mailing you a copy of a report and the location of some personnel files you need to read right now.

Sam frowned at the screen, wondering for the hundredth time how Mac always had access to classified information.

He reached into his desk and pulled out his CAC card reader, along with his military ID. He shoved the ID into the slot and opened his e-mail. The message from Mac sent his heart pounding in his ears.

Here's the preliminary report on what happened in Kabul. For further details, follow this link.

Sam opened the file and stared at the document. At the top was a date he'd remember for the rest of his life. The day in Kabul when his whole life changed forever. A chill ran up Sam's spine when he clicked through to the dot-mil page Mac had indicated. His hands felt numb as he stroked the gun with an oilcloth.

He didn't need to read the report to remember. It was painted on the inside of his brain.

His commanding officer had ordered him to a warehouse in Kabul. It was early morning, but the village had already been bustling with vendors hawking bread and mothers hustling young children into shops and schools and banks. The smell of raw sewage drifted in through an open window, and Sam squinted against the blinding sunlight.

He had only sparse details on his target. White shirt.

Slight limp. Gray backpack. Known terrorist who had to be neutralized at once.

That was Sam's job. As one of the top snipers in the Marines, he'd been called on to perform it countless times. His commanding officer had given the time and place, but no further detail, save one:

Shoot to kill.

Sam had every intention of doing it. He'd done it before, expected he'd be doing it again and again through more tours of duty.

Then he saw the face in his scope. The target.

A boy?

He couldn't have been more than ten years old, eleven at the most. Sam watched, hesitating, finger on the trigger. The boy looked up, not at Sam, but at a flock of birds fluttering overhead. The kid smiled—the gap-toothed smile of a boy on Christmas morning, and Sam felt something inside him twist.

"Take the shot!" his commanding officer shouted through his earpiece.

Sam watched as the boy took something out of his pocket—candy?—and smiled again.

"Take the shot!"

No!

Sweat beaded on Sam's forehead, and his finger twitched on the trigger. He hesitated—for seconds? Minutes? He wasn't sure.

Whatever it was, it was too long.

The blast had come instantly, a blinding shower of hot glass and screaming voices and acrid smoke.

Suicide bomber.

The words had pulsed through Sam's brain as he covered his head with his arms, blocking pieces of flying glass and the screams of the victims. He still heard the screams now, still smelled the smoke and felt the sharp sting of hot stone shards piercing his skin.

Sam shook his head to clear the memory, forcing himself to study the report Mac had sent. Then he followed the trail to the personnel files, the words coming at him in a fuzzy jumble.

Timing device.
Casualties unavoidable.
Officer Samuel R. Kercher found not at fault.

Sam blinked, trying to understand what he was reading. Beside him on the desk, his phone buzzed. He glanced down at it. *Mac.*

"Hello?"

"Did you get it?" Mac demanded.

"Get what?"

"The report. I can see you've logged in, Sam—don't play dumb."

Sam swallowed, his eyes still glued to the screen. "I'm looking at it now."

"Then you know." Mac's voice was low and oddly soothing. Sam wondered where the hell he was and how he had access to all this information.

"Know what?" Sam asked. "I don't understand."

Mac cleared his throat. "You know what the rest of us have been trying to tell you for weeks, Sam. It wasn't your goddamn fault."

"How—"

"The bomber was wired with a timer set to blow at a precise moment. There wasn't a damn thing you could have done differently to change that."

"But if I'd put a bullet between his eyes—"

"It wouldn't have mattered. Whether you'd obeyed the order to fire, or hesitated in taking the shot or put down your weapon and played the fiddle while juggling oranges with your feet—none of it would have changed the outcome one bit."

Sam sat silent, digesting the information. So it wasn't his fault. All these weeks of assuming the worst, of questioning his abilities as a soldier and a protector and a man—

"I'm not a total fuckup then."

"No shit, Sherlock. I could have told you that. You think I'd have you looking out for my sister if I didn't believe you were the best man for the job?"

"No," Sam said slowly, gripping the phone tighter. "Still, I failed to follow orders."

"There are worse things in the world than that, Sam."

The words hung there between them for a moment, and he wondered just how much Mac really knew. Maybe everything. Did it matter?

Sam stayed silent a moment, digesting the information. He wasn't responsible for all those innocent deaths. He hadn't screwed up—not completely, anyway. He was a good protector—a good soldier.

A good man.

"Look, Mac, I've gotta go."

"Call me after you've read everything," Mac said. "To-morrow if you need time to process it."

"I'll do that. And Mac? One more thing."

"What's that?"

"What you just said about there being worse things than not following orders?" Sam took a steadying breath. "I'm in love with your sister. I don't give a shit how overprotective you are or if you gut me with your field knife. I love her and I want to protect her and be with her and fight for her if I have to."

It was Mac's turn to be silent. It could be a bad sign, but Sam hoped it wasn't.

"You there, Mac?"

He grunted. "We'll talk about this when I get to town."

"When's that?"

"I'll let you know when I arrive."

Mac disconnected the call, and Sam resisted the urge to smile. He'd done it. He'd come clean with Mac.

But more importantly, he'd cleared his name. Not just his name, but his conscience. All this time with Sheri and the boys, he'd been proving to himself that he had it in him to serve and protect. To succeed where he'd failed before, albeit in a slightly different setting.

Maybe it was time to forgive himself.

A wave of ridiculous relief washed over him. He looked down at the gun in his lap, polished to perfection. He glanced back at the computer screen, reading the words more slowly this time.

The incident that occurred at 0800 hours in the warehouse beside Al-Aaimmani Mosque in Kabul has been determined to be—

"Sam?"

Her voice jolted him from his reverie. He turned to see her fingers curled around the door he'd left ajar, to see her pushing it open in slow motion.

Fuck.

He looked down at the pistol in his lap, at his military ID in the CAC reader, at the tremble in his own hands, and knew it was all over.

Chapter Twenty

Sam's heart skidded to a halt in his chest. He didn't breathe. He didn't blink. He didn't say a word as Sheri stared him down with the stoniest expression he'd ever seen in his life.

She folded her arms over her chest and looked him dead in the eye. "Were you planning to tell me?"

He didn't reply, knowing anything he could possibly say would be useless.

Tell you what? would earn him a well-deserved punch in the jaw. *Yes* or *no* wasn't the right answer either, so he stayed silent, hating Mac, hating Jonathan, mostly hating himself.

He looked down at the gun in his lap, then at the laptop screen. He hadn't been fast enough to hide either one.

Nice fucking sniper reflexes, asshole.

"Sheri, I can explain," he began, even though he couldn't. Not really.

And she knew it. She gave a hollow little laugh and shook her head. "Oh really? I'd love to hear you explain it.

Tell me all about how a big, strapping Marine came to be my goddamn manny."

Sam swallowed. "Did Jonathan tell you?"

She flinched, and he instantly regretted his words.

"My ex-husband knew? Are you fucking kidding me?"

Her voice was nearly a shriek now, and Sam said a grateful prayer the boys were heavy sleepers. Sheri stepped into the room and began pacing like a woman on the brink of throwing something. Sam didn't blame her.

"Jonathan guessed," Sam said, wondering if that made a difference. "And Mac knew, of course. And Grant, and—"

"You have to be joking," she snapped. "Everyone under the sun knew but me? My goddamn ex-husband? My brothers? That guy at the beach today, for fuck's sake. That's what that was all about, right? You went there to spy on me, and he recognized you. Is that how it happened?"

He had to admire her powers of deduction. He stayed silent, wishing like hell there was something he could say to make this go away. The sick feeling in his gut told him that wouldn't be happening anytime soon.

Her eyes dropped to the CAC reader, then to the gun in his lap. She gave a furious little laugh.

"Nice gun. I'd say that's a Marine-issued Colt .45 Close Quarter Battle Pistol with a custom trigger, manual safety, and glowing Tritium sights for low-light conditions."

"How did you—?"

"I'm a firearm geek, Sam. I was a military wife, for chrissakes. And a military sister, and a military daughter. I've spent my whole goddamn life eating, sleeping, breathing, and drinking military trivia. I probably know more about the goddamn Marines than you do."

"That's likely," he said, feeling stupid for ever thinking he could pull the wool over her eyes. Feeling ashamed for even trying.

"Let me see your shoulder."

"What?"

"Take off your goddamn shirt and turn around."

Not sure what else to do, he complied. He turned slowly, braced for her to hit or punch or kick. He had no doubt he deserved it.

"Teufelshunde," she said softly. "That's your tattoo. Devil dog, the unofficial mascot of the United States Marine Corps. Half the men in my family had it on bumper stickers and T-shirts, for chrissakes. I'm such an idiot."

"No," Sam said, turning back around. "You're not an idiot. Whatever you take away from this, don't let it be that."

She shook her head, blinking back tears. "I trusted you."

"Let me explain."

"I thought you were different. But you're not. You're just like they are."

He wasn't sure who "they" were, but he knew he shouldn't be flattered by the comparison. He knew he should defend himself, but he honest to God couldn't come up with one thing to say in his own defense.

"I never wanted to hurt you," he said. "And I didn't want to deceive you."

"No? Well congratulations, Sam. You've gone and accomplished two things you didn't set out to do. You deserve a fucking medal."

"I was just following Mac's orders—"

"With no thought at all to *my* feelings?" She shook her head. "I was betrayed once by a controlling military jerk,

Sam. I wanted better for my boys. For *me*. Following orders is no excuse for lying. For pretending to be honorable when you're anything but."

Sam swallowed as the words struck a nerve. "I did it to protect you. To keep my word to Mac. To help you when I knew you wouldn't want to accept help from someone like me."

She rolled her eyes. "Spare me. I don't need protection or help, I need honesty. You pretended to be someone you weren't. You let me trust you, Sam. Do you have any idea what it's like to trust again after your husband betrays you?"

He shook his head and struggled to come up with something comforting to say. There was nothing.

His eyes slipped to the laptop on his desk. To the words that said he'd been cleared of any wrongdoing.

Did it even matter now?

He looked back at Sheri.

"I'm sorry."

"Get out," she said. "I want you out of the house by morning."

"Sheri, please." He stepped toward her, aching to take her into his arms and make everything okay again.

She took two steps back. "You lied to me. Just like Jonathan. And you conspired with my stupid brothers and my stupid ex to turn me into a fool."

"We were just protecting you, Sheri. That's what this was all about. What everyone wanted. We just wanted to keep you safe."

She shook her head, her expression fierce. "You wanted to keep me locked in a cage. You wanted to control me like every other asshole military douchebag in my life. You thought you could decide all by yourself what's best for me, and keep me in the dark." She took a breath, her shoulders sagging. "There's no room in my life for liars, Sam. And there's no room in the boys' lives for men who set that sort of example. I want you out of my house and out of my life for good."

"But the boys." He swallowed back the lump in his throat at the thought of never seeing them again. It hurt almost as much as the idea of life without Sheri. "Who's going to watch the boys?"

"I'll figure it out. I'll take time off work or beg my mom to come or work out something with Kelli. I don't know yet, but it's not your concern."

He swallowed again, fighting to think of any other defense he might be able to offer. Everything sounded futile. Everything but the truth.

And there was still that.

"I love you," he said, and the words sounded right the instant they left his lips, so he swallowed and tried again with more conviction. "*I love you.*"

She shook her head and turned away. "I can't believe a single word you say."

She walked out of the room, leaving a chill in her wake.

• • •

Sheri stared glumly into her empty teacup the next afternoon and sighed.

"We're skipping the tea this time and going straight for the bourbon," Kelli said, sloshing a healthy serving into Sheri's mug before pouring some into her own and taking a seat at the dining room table.

Sheri looked around the room, trying not to cry. On the floor near the door was one of the beanie peacocks Sam had bought for the boys, its head cocked at a jaunty angle. At the edge of the counter sat a turquoise dish towel with a singed edge, the casualty of one of Sam's attempts at dinner. A cookbook sat open beside the stove, its pages splattered with something green.

Sheri shook her head. "At least it all makes sense now."

"What makes sense?" Kelli said, taking a sip from her mug and making a face.

"Why he wasn't all that great in the kitchen."

"As long as he was good in the bedroom, did it really matter?"

Sheri frowned and took a drink. "That's not helping."

"Try a bigger sip."

"No, I mean reminding me I slept with Sam. With a man I didn't know at all. Another knuckle-dragging military jerk who lied to me. Don't you find the pattern disturbing?"

Kelli shrugged, considering the question. "Not really. I mean, we all have our types. Your brother, for instance. Emotionally unavailable egomaniac who doesn't know I'm alive—totally my type. When are you fixing us up?"

Sheri rolled her eyes and took a bigger sip of her drink. It burned all the way down, but Kelli had a point. It did make her feel better. "The only way I'd fix you up with my brother at this point is if you pledged to cut off his testicles while he slept. Seriously, after what he did to me—"

"What exactly did he do to you?" Kelli interrupted, swirling her finger around the top of her mug. "I mean, I'm mad because you're mad, and I'll insult the genitals of every male on the planet if it'll help. But I'm not sure I understand what your brother did that was so awful."

"He lied to me," Sheri snapped. "He said he scoured the ends of the earth to hire the best possible nanny, and that Sam was it."

"Well, he kinda was, wasn't he? I mean, the boys loved him."

I *loved him*, Sheri thought, then wanted to scrub her brain with a Brillo pad. Where the hell had that come from?

"Mac knew I was done with overbearing military assholes, and knew I didn't want some meathead like that watching over me," Sheri said. "So what did he do? He lied to me and hired the meathead anyway, and they all played me like a fool." She blinked back tears of betrayal, tears that tasted just like the ones she'd cried when Jonathan left. "They all lied to me—Jonathan, Mac, Sam—every single one of them."

Kelli set her mug down and reached for Sheri's hand, giving it a comforting squeeze. "Honey, you're my very best friend, and you know I've got your back through anything. And I know it sucks feeling like everyone but you was in on the scam. Even your idiot ex, for crying out loud. That's lousy, no doubt about it."

"But?" Sheri prompted, bracing herself for a dose of Kelli's tough love.

"*But*, do you think it's possible Sam and your brother deserve the benefit of the doubt here?"

"No."

"I'm glad you're keeping an open mind."

Sheri shook her head and began breaking pieces off an oatmeal cookie on the plate between them. Sam had made the cookies the day before, accidentally using salt instead of sugar. They tasted like hell, but she couldn't stop eating them.

"Look, all I'm saying is that your brothers wanted to protect you," Kelli said. "They may have been a little misguided and ass-hatty about it, but they had your best interests at heart. And Sam was just stuck between a rock and a hard place."

"Sam's *hard place* is part of what caused this whole mess."

"Stop that," Kelli said, smacking the back of her hand. "If I remember the story correctly, *you're* the one who pulled him into the shower with you. *You're* the one who dropped to your knees because of a bunch of closet shelves. *You're* the one who took off your robe in his room yesterday morning."

Sheri shoved the cookie aside and scowled at her friend. "You know that part about me feeling foolish? This isn't helping."

"You weren't foolish. You were attracted to a smart, strong, sexy, competent man who was good to your children. There are worse things in life, you know."

Sheri scowled, hating the fact that a tiny part of her knew Kelli was right. Watching Sam pack his bags had been ten times more heart-wrenching than watching Jonathan do the same damn thing six months ago. Watching him tuck those little beanie peacocks into the crook of each boy's arm had completely undone her.

"There's definitely a pattern here," Sheri said, dabbing at her eyes as she spotted the second beanie peacock under her chair. She kicked it across the room and looked back at

Kelli. "I keep falling for the same macho assholes over and over."

Kelli snorted. "Sam has about as much in common with your ex as a doughnut has in common with a bike tire. I can tell you right now which one belongs in your mouth and which should be ground into the pavement, and it's not the doughnut."

"You have a way with words," Sheri admitted, feeling a surge of affection for her friend despite the fact that Kelli wasn't exactly giving her the sympathetic butt-pats she'd hoped for. "I should probably wake up the boys."

"How long have they been napping?"

"Awhile. Sam insisted on waking them up when he left to say good-bye. I'm not sure they understood, but they've been crying and fidgety all day, so I think they know something's going on."

"Any idea where Sam went?"

"No."

"Do you think he just got on a plane and left?"

She shrugged. "That's what I told him to do."

"Does he usually follow your orders?"

"Depends on whether I'm naked. At least, it used to."

Kelli squeezed her hand again and stood up. "I should probably get home. You sure you don't want me to go grab some things and stay the night? We can make brownies and drink bourbon and insult penises."

"Tempting, but no. I need to get used to being on my own."

"Is your mom going to come over from Honolulu?"

Sheri nodded. "She offered to help me find a new nanny. And she promised to send Mac to bed without supper the next time she sees him."

Kelli gave a firm nod. "Hopefully he'll learn a lesson from all this."

Sheri sighed. "I know I did."

"Not to blow the nanny 'til you've frisked him for firearms?"

"Make that two lessons."

Kelli smiled and patted her on the shoulder. "You'll be okay, Sher. You're a great mom, a great friend, and if the look on Sam's face as he was leaving was any indication, a great lay."

"Thanks, Kelli. And thanks for bringing lunch."

Kelli stepped close and pulled her into a warm embrace that smelled like jasmine and puppy breath. "I'll be at the clinic late tonight doing lab work on a bunch of endangered tortoises we seized from a private collection. Call if you need anything."

Sheri nodded against her friend's shoulder, trying not to get snot on her. She'd been holding back the tears all day, but as Kelli rocked her back and forth in a supportive hug, she felt them prick the corners of her eyes again.

"You'd better get going," she said, pulling back and moving toward the kitchen with the teacups. "Thanks again, Kel."

"My pleasure. Be strong, babe."

Kelli stooped down and picked up the beanie peacock, setting it gently on the accent table beside the door. She turned one last time and blew Sheri a kiss before walking out into the bright sunlight.

Sheri took a steadying breath as the door closed behind her best friend. She scrubbed her hands over her face and wondered for the hundredth time where Sam had gone.

"Enough," she ordered herself, and went to take a shower.

Her visions of a long, leisurely cry beneath the hot spray were cut short by the boys wailing over the baby monitor, which was just as well. The last thing she needed was the opportunity to picture every nook and cranny of the shower where Sam had explored every nook and cranny of her body.

With her hair still unwashed and her body wrapped in hastily donned jersey shorts and a button-up tank top she was pretty sure she'd buttoned crookedly, Sheri bounced Jackson in her arms while gently rocking Jeffrey's little carrier with her bare foot.

"Shhhh," she whispered, bouncing harder. "Mommy's here."

Jackson wailed harder, and Sheri wondered if he was thinking about Sam. He screwed up his tiny face and made a loud *pfft* noise, then crapped his pants.

"My thoughts exactly," Sheri said, and bent to the task of changing him.

The day dragged on, with Sheri growing increasingly despondent and exhausted. The boys fluctuated wildly between exuberant joy and tired crankiness, yanking Sheri's mood along with them. While Jackson gummed his beanie peacock, Jeffrey sneezed a mixture of rice cereal and carrot all over her hair.

She didn't bother to clean it off.

By the time she had both boys latched into their car seats, it was already getting dark. She drove to the grocery store with her iPod playing the dirty, raw Southern rock of Kings of Leon, singing along to "The End" while she blinked back stupid tears.

"It won't be long before you guys are going to understand

lyrics, and then we'll have to play 'Wheels on the Bus' on an endless loop," she called into the backseat.

Jackson hiccupped and threw his teething ring on the floor. Jeffrey blew a snot bubble.

"God, I love you guys," she sniffed, and parked the car in front of Safeway. She turned around to look at them, her heart ripping in half as she took in their chubby cheeks and bare baby toes. "Look, I know I'm not the best mom in the world, and you guys kinda got the short end of the stick here. But you know I'd do anything for you, right?"

Jackson hooted and smacked his hand on the arm of his car seat. Jeffrey stuck his fist in his mouth and kicked his little bare legs.

"And you know Sam is crazy about you, too," she said. "It's just that sometimes, people lie, and they aren't who they say they are, and they have to go away."

Bored with his fist, Jeffrey attempted to shove his foot in his mouth, while Jackson threw his pacifier on the floor.

"Good talk, guys," Sheri said, and picked up the pacifier.

The grocery shopping took her three times longer than she'd hoped, and she was drained by the time she hauled four big sacks of groceries, packed tightly in the shopping cart around the boys' carriers, back to the car.

"This was easier with another set of hands," she muttered, and tried not to think of Sam's hands.

She latched the boys back in their seats, loaded the groceries into the trunk, and drove slowly back home with the stereo at a slightly more soothing volume and her headlights slicing through the darkness.

By the time she pulled into the driveway, she was giving serious thought to leaving the food in the trunk and just going straight to bed.

"Not an option in Hawaii," she muttered, unbuckling her seat belt as she stepped out of the car. "Not unless I want my perishables to perish and my frozen goods to unfreeze."

She unbuckled Jeffrey first, then Jackson, maneuvering their car seats Transformer-style to become baby carriers. Jackson reached up and grabbed the front of her tank top, his tiny fist fastening on the top button with a viselike grip.

"Honey, no," she murmured, but she was too late.

She heard the rip of fabric and the skitter of buttons popping off one by one to roll down the concrete driveway. She glanced down, trying to figure out how much boob she was showing and whether the shirt could be salvaged.

Did it matter now? There was no one around to notice, to tease or ogle or offer to fix it while she fought tooth and nail to avoid taking help from anyone.

She sighed and hoisted the baby carriers, one on each arm. They were almost too big for her to lug like this, though Sam had made it look easy. How the hell was she going to manage this as a single mom? She'd done it before, in the six months between Jonathan's leaving and Sam's showing up. But things were different now. It was partly that the boys were getting bigger, but that wasn't all.

There was a Sam-sized hole in her life, and she knew it wasn't just the child-care help she missed.

She marched up to the front porch gripping a baby carrier in each hand, leaving the groceries for the second run. She set both carriers down on the bottom step and stuck her key in the lock. It turned easily—too easily—and Sheri muttered to herself as she shoved the door open with her hip.

"Gotta get better about making sure that's locked," she

told the boys as she picked up their carriers and lugged them into the house.

She moved through the foyer in darkness, carting the boys to the center of the living room. She set them down there, then turned back to the entry table to drop her keys in the little dish. She spotted the beanie peacock there and fought the wistful pang that gripped her gut. She thought about throwing it in the trash, but couldn't bring herself to do it.

She turned to the boys. "I'll be right back, guys. Gotta grab the groceries. Don't move."

Sheri hurried out the door, hating to leave them alone for even an instant, but knowing she didn't have a choice. She hefted the four bags out of the trunk and hurried back up the walkway, wondering whether she'd be smarter to tackle the groceries or the requisite diaper change for Jeffrey first.

She hustled back into the house and kicked off her shoes at the door, relieved to feel the cool floor under her bare feet. She set the groceries on the floor and turned to find the light switch. She froze with her hand midway to it, her eyes fixing on the stupid peacock.

She reached for it, wanting to touch it one more time, to remember Sam's kindness and understanding. To recall the look on his face when he'd called her beautiful, smart, funny, a good mother.

A sound snapped her attention back to the moment. She looked up, squinting toward the dark hallway on the other side of the living room.

The figure loomed in the shadows, his face masked in darkness, as he moved slowly, ominously toward her.

Toward her babies.

In a flash of moonlight, she saw the gun glinting in his hand.

Chapter Twenty-One

Sheri gasped as the figure stepped out of the shadows. Her heart pounded in her ears and the familiar scent of his cologne made her stomach churn.

"Jonathan. How the hell did you get in here?"

"Sheridan," he said, stepping into place behind the boys' carriers as he held the pistol in one hand like a pageant prop. "Good to see you again. I've been getting acquainted with our new home. It's a nice place."

She swallowed, tasting bile. How had she ever loved this man? "You're insane. How did you get in?"

"First thing we're going to do after I move in is install new locks on the doors. It's much too easy to break in." He looked down at the gun in his hand and shook his head. "The second thing we're going to do is have fewer secrets between us. This gun, for instance."

"My collection of heirloom firearms was never a secret, you jerk," she snapped. "You knew about them. They belong to my family."

"And as your husband, *I'm* your family. Keeping your valuables under lock and key the way you always used to—well, that's going to change now. So is your repertoire of recipes. You're not still making that potato flake chicken, are you?"

Sheri took a step forward, her eyes flicking between the baby carriers, the gun, and the menacing look on her ex-husband's face. "What I do with my personal possessions and what I make for dinner are none of your business. Get away from my babies."

He snorted. "They're my children, Sheridan. I have every right to take them."

"*Take* them? Take them where?"

Her voice was practically a shriek, but Jonathan looked unfazed. "You've been ignoring and disrespecting me long enough. It's time I took some action. I want us to be a family again, and the only way you're going to listen to me is if I have your children. *Our* children."

She took another step toward him, her gut twisting in fury and disgust. "Get away from them."

Jonathan raised the pistol. "No, you get away. Don't come any closer. I've already packed a bag for you, Sheridan. You're going to turn around now and walk back out to the car. And for God's sake, put down that stupid toy. I already threw some things in a bag for the boys, they'll be fine."

Sheri looked down at her own hands, surprised to discover she'd picked up the beanie peacock. She blinked at it as her mind flashed to Sam, wondering where he was and whether she'd ever see him again. She gripped the toy tighter and looked up at her ex. As her eyes locked with his, she took another step toward him.

"You're crazy," she hissed. "How did I never see that before?"

His finger touched the trigger on the pistol. "Stay right there, Sheridan."

Her heart bumped hard against her rib cage as she took a steadying breath and one more step forward. She looked down at her babies. Jackson waved one chubby hand in the air, oblivious to the danger pulsing through the room.

"Don't come any closer," he barked. "Turn around and walk to the car. *Now!*"

Disobeying his order, she took another step forward, close enough to stretch out and touch his sleeve if she wanted. She shuddered at the thought of touching him and met his eyes instead.

"I'm warning you, Sheridan," he shouted.

Jeffrey squawked in alarm. Jackson whimpered, his soft snuffles signaling the start of a full-fledged crying jag. Sheri took another step forward, needing to reach her boys, needing to make sure they were okay—

"Stop right there!" he barked. He held the gun on Sheri for two more beats, then turned and pointed it at the babies.

Sheri lunged, pouncing on him with every ounce of mama-bear fury she never knew she had. She smacked the peacock against the side of his head, remembering what her father had taught her in a self-defense lesson at age eight. *Strike hard and from above.*

Her weapon left something to be desired, but she had the element of surprise on her side. Jonathan stepped back as she hit him across the eyes. His foot tangled with the second peacock lying facedown on the carpet, and he tripped.

Staggering, he fell to his knees. She raised the peacock again as Jonathan lifted the pistol.

He blinked at her, dazed. "Drop the—the—what the hell is that?"

She hit him again, once more in the face and then in the arm. He kept his grip on the gun, but he was still on his knees, so she kicked him hard in the ribs. She delivered one more smack with the peacock, throwing every ounce of strength into the blow as he toppled sideways.

"Lesson number one," she hissed, kicking him in the groin this time. "Don't ever, *ever* threaten my children."

He dropped the pistol, and she kicked it away, her fingers still gripping the peacock. "And lesson number two," she snarled. "If you're going to point a gun at someone raised in a family of gun nuts, make sure it's not her grandfather's blowback-operated, semiautomatic FN Model 1910 pistol that hasn't worked since World War II. There's a reason I never let you touch it, asshole—it's an antique."

She drew her foot back to kick him again, then stopped herself. He was already down, and her babies were safe. She shook her head in disgust. "Don't you ever, *ever,* touch me, my children, or my family heirlooms again."

She dropped to her knees beside him, grabbing his wrists and jerking them behind his back. With one hand, she yanked Sam's makeshift teething ring holder off the handle of Jeffrey's carrier. She used it to cinch Jonathan's wrists behind his back, then leaned over the boys to make sure they were okay.

"Hey, guys," she whispered, her voice shaking. "Everything's fine now. Mama's got you."

She stroked a finger over Jeffrey's cheek, and he stopped

whimpering at once. She moved to Jackson, wiping his little nose with the back of her hand. "Shhh," she soothed. "You're okay now. Everything's all over."

"Not entirely," said a voice in the darkness.

Sheri snapped her head up and blinked.

A man in black stepped through the front door. Shadows fell behind him as he strode slowly toward her.

Chapter Twenty-Two

"Mac!" Sheri screamed, leaping to her feet and launching herself across the room at her brother. "Ohmygod, why are you here?"

"To offer you protection." He glanced at the prone figure on the ground and frowned. "Something you don't appear to need at the moment."

"Protection? Protection from what?"

Mac stooped down and studied Jonathan, checking to be sure his wrists were secure. Then he grabbed him by the hair and brought his face down close.

"You were never good enough for her," Mac said calmly. "Now that you've answered to her, you're going to answer to me."

He thrust Jonathan away and glanced at each of the babies, ensuring everyone was safe. Then he stood up and turned to face his sister.

"Sam called me after you kicked him out," Mac said.

"Said he was worried about Jonathan showing up and doing something stupid. He said if you wouldn't let him watch over you, he wanted me here to do it for him. I moved up the date of my visit to be here in his place."

Sheri swallowed, feeling hollow all of a sudden. "Sam called you?"

"And I've called the police. They should be here momentarily, so let's clear up a few things before they arrive, shall we?"

Sheri opened her mouth to speak—to tell her brother what she thought about his conniving, lying, manipulative behavior—but Mac grabbed her hand and leveled her with a steely stare.

"*You* are not speaking. You're listening. And here's what I have to say to you." Mac caught her other hand, his grip warm and loving while his eyes flashed cold in the dim light of the house. Sheri realized it was one of the few times in her adult life she'd seen her brother without sunglasses, even at night.

"Number one," Mac said. "You are a good mother. An *amazing* mother, and if your demonstration of pure, primal maternal instinct just now didn't prove that to you, you need to seriously reevaluate your judgment."

Sheri swallowed, struck speechless by his words. "How did you know?"

"I know everything, Sheri. This bullshit I've been hearing from Sam about your certainty you lack some 'mommy chip'—that stops *now*."

"But—"

"Number two," Mac said, ignoring her feeble attempt at protest as he gripped her hands harder. "Sam is a good

Marine, a good man, and a good friend who did his best to return a favor to me. What I asked him to do was watch out for my beautiful, competent, overachieving, stubborn-as-fuck sister. Did he, or did he not do that?"

Sheri felt her eyes filling with tears. She thought about the last twenty-four hours, about her chaotic day without Sam around to laugh with or cook with or tend to her babies with his offbeat brand of caregiver instinct. She swallowed again, picturing his face in her mind, remembering the feel of his hands on her body, the smell of his skin against hers.

Did she *need* a man in her life?

Maybe not. But she sure as hell wanted one. Her life certainly felt richer and more joyful with Sam in it.

"Is he still on island?" she whispered, her eyes fixed on her brother's.

Mac nodded once, curtly. "I believe so. I can't say for certain where. His plane doesn't leave until morning."

Sheri stepped back, her stomach flipping over in her abdomen as her heart began to race. "I have to find him."

"Why?"

"I have to tell him I'm sorry and that I understand now and that I want to make love to him forever and—wait, why am I telling you?"

"I have no idea."

"Can you watch the boys, please?"

"The police will be here any minute," Mac said. "Don't you think you should wait?"

"You can explain." She scanned the room feverishly, looking for her purse. She couldn't find it, but she spotted her phone on the table and grabbed that. "You're good at handling authority figures, just tell them I had to run out.

And, um—try not to kill Jonathan."

"Where are you going?"

"To find Sam," Sheri said, already moving toward the door. "To throw myself at him and beg him to come back and make a life with the boys and with me."

"Sheri?"

"Don't try to stop me, Mac."

"I wouldn't dream of it. But don't you think you should put on some shoes? Maybe a shirt that's not ripped open?"

But Sheri was already out the door, car keys in her hand, an idea forming in the back of her brain where Sam might have gone.

Please say it's not too late.

She tried his number once, twice, three times while she drove, but the call just went to voicemail. Was the phone dead, or was he just ignoring her calls?

Either way, she had to find him. She had to tell him what she'd realized.

She careened into the parking lot at Smith's Tropical Paradise. There were plenty of cars in the lot, though she couldn't pick out his Jeep anywhere. Still she had to try.

She sprinted to the gate, barely noticing the gravel biting into her bare feet, the breeze through her half-buttoned top, the chunk of carrot in her hair that smacked her in the face as she ran.

The smell of tropical flowers and river water was heavy in the air, and a light breeze tousled her curls, reminding her she hadn't combed her hair for God knows how long.

As she approached the gate, an attendant stepped forward in a grass skirt and coconut bra. The woman looked at Sheri, her eyes traveling from the torn shirt to the crazy hair to the crazier eyes. Sheri brushed a hand over her cheek and felt something crusted there, oatmeal, probably.

Christ, had she even looked in a mirror today?

"Sorry ma'am," the attendant said, not unkindly. "The park closed at four. Only luau guests at this point."

Sheri looked down at her disheveled appearance. She was hardly dressed for dinner and a show, so she couldn't blame the woman for assuming the worst.

"Please," Sheri begged, spitting a carrot-caked curl out of her mouth. "There's a man."

The woman smiled, understanding flickering across her features. "There always is."

"No, I mean—inside. I think. I need to go find him. I need to tell him—"

"I understand, but I can't let you in without a ticket."

"I'll buy a ticket!" She looked down, realizing she'd left her purse, her driver's license, her credit cards, her shoes— hell, pretty much everything, including her sanity—at home.

She didn't even have lipstick to make a good impression, but that was the least of her concerns right now. She had to find Sam.

She looked back at the woman and felt the tears prick the back of her throat. There had to be a way.

"Please," she whispered. "This might be my only chance with him."

The woman's face softened. "Tell you what. I'm a sucker for a good love story, and I can see you're having a rough night. Go find your man. Come back tomorrow and pay for a ticket. And if it works out, you have your wedding here."

Relief flooded her whole body, coursing through her veins to mix with the adrenaline. "I promise," Sheri whispered, knowing for certain it was a promise she meant to keep. "You're an angel. An angel in a coconut bra."

"That's the best kind of angel," the woman said, and stepped aside to let Sheri pass. Sheri rushed by her, gravel and discarded bird seed biting into her feet.

"You want a brush or something, honey?"

"No time!" Sheri called as she moved through the entrance, her eyes already scanning the grounds for signs of Sam.

She sprinted across the grass toward a group of tiki torches near a large hut. A cluster of peacocks scattered, squawking their displeasure at her disruption. Hawaiian music lilted on the breeze, and she inhaled the rich smell of smoked pork. Her gut twisted a little at that as she thought of Sam and the burned dinner and how much she wanted him around to burn dinners forever and ever.

She tripped over something that might have been a coconut or a rooster, but she kept going. She didn't care. All she cared about was finding Sam and telling him she loved him. That she understood now what he'd been trying to do.

Her eyes scanned the crowd milling around outside the hut. A few people stopped and stared, probably wondering about the crazy-eyed, food-covered, half-dressed woman barging in on their special event.

Sheri didn't care.

Dinner must've ended, but the show hadn't started yet. Was he even here? Had her instincts led her wrong? It wouldn't be the first time. Maybe this was a dumb idea. Maybe she shouldn't have come. Maybe—

She spotted him against a row of tiki torches. At least she thought it was him. It was definitely a big guy with rumpled hair that curled at the collar, his massive shoulders silhouetted by torch flames and smoke from the fire pits. He was tossing handfuls of birdseed to a cluster of peacocks who pecked and squawked and strutted at his feet.

She couldn't see his face, but she was sure it was him. She'd know that body anywhere.

"Sam!"

He turned slowly, his face registering surprise, then shock as his eyes found hers. Sheri reached up to smooth her frizzed hair, to adjust the torn shirt, to wipe the smears of food off her face.

To hell with it.

She dropped her hands and stepped forward, determined not to be self-conscious. Determined to say what she needed to say. She took a shaky breath and met his eyes.

"I want to talk to you about lying."

His face creased with guilt and disappointment. "Sheri, I'm sorry I hurt you. I'm sorry I did it so soon after you had your heart ripped out by another dishonest bastard. I know what you said about lying. That it's the absolute worst thing. Worse than riptides and parking tickets and pubic lice and —"

"I said that?"

He nodded once. "Something like that."

She stepped closer, shivering a little in the night air as she folded her arms over her torn shirt. "I'm sure I said that. I'm sure I even meant it at the time. But here's the thing I've realized about lying — sometimes, people have good reasons for doing it."

"What?" Sam blinked, his eyes flickering with firelight.

"I'm not talking about cheaters who lie to stick their

dick in a stripper," she said. Her voice carried farther than she meant it to, and a few luau guests turned to stare. She pressed on, determined to make this right. To say what she needed to say.

"I'm talking about self-preservation," she said, not sure she was getting the words quite right. "I'm talking about lies to protect someone or help someone who won't accept help or to be true to a friend or yourself or to—"

"Sheri," he said, taking another step forward and reaching out to catch her hands in his. The warmth of them gave her strength, though his eyes were questioning. "What on God's green earth are you talking about?"

"I'm saying sometimes lying *isn't* the worst thing," she said, clenching his fingers in hers as a curl of smoke stung her eyes. Or maybe it was a tear of emotion, she wasn't sure. "I'm saying I weigh ten pounds more than I admitted on my driver's license. I'm saying I color my hair because I started going gray before the twins were born. I'm saying I wear Spanx under a cocktail dress, and that I haven't really read *War and Peace* even though I meant to. I'm saying I didn't tell you Jonathan was harassing me because I was scared and didn't want to admit that, not even to myself. I'm saying I ate the last Twinkie but told you it was Kelli, and I'm saying that personal massager under my bed isn't really for neck pain. I'm saying—"

"Sheri," he said, his eyes flickering with more than fire-light now. There was humor there. And love. It definitely looked like love.

"I love you," she said, wanting to make sure she said it before he could. "I love you and I want you and I need you and I don't want you to go. That's what I'm trying to say."

He smiled, the first time she'd seen him do it since last night. It was the most beautiful sight she'd ever seen, and she felt herself crumpling into him. He caught her in his strong hands, his body supporting hers, his arms folding around her and engulfing her in the sweetest, warmest embrace she'd ever felt.

"I love you, too," he whispered. "And don't take this the wrong way, but you kinda smell like baby vomit."

She drew back, laughing, and looked into his eyes. "So do you. And it's the best thing I've ever smelled in my whole life."

Chapter Twenty-Three

When they returned to the house, Mac was reading the boys a bedtime story.

"…and this type of flak vest is designed to provide protection from case fragments, high-explosive weaponry, antiaircraft artillery, grenades, and some types of shot used in shotguns and land mines, though it is not designed to— Hey, Sam, hey Sheri. What's up?"

Mac smiled at them both, though his eyes held Sheri's with a question. She smiled back and squeezed Sam's hand before stepping forward to greet her brother.

"What are you read— Never mind." She dropped to her knees in front of him and hugged her babies one at a time. Then she looked up at Mac. "Thank you for watching them."

"My pleasure."

"Where's Jonathan?"

"He's been dealt with." Mac pressed his lips together, the familiar signal he was done discussing a subject. "I take it from the glow on your faces things went well?"

She grinned. "You can take it from the glow on our faces that we just had sex in the car."

Mac closed the book in his lap. "I didn't need to know that."

Sam stepped forward and helped Sheri to her feet again. "Well, here's something you do need to know, Mac. Your sister and I are together and in love. Deal with it."

Mac stood, his expression surprisingly warm, as he shook Sam's hand. "Congratulations, Sam. You're getting the best girl in the world." He turned to her, leaning in for a hug. "Congratulations, Sher."

Sheri let him pull her into a hug for a moment before drawing back. "Wait a minute." She looked her brother in the eye, brimming with equal parts love and annoyance. "This is for tricking me."

She punched him squarely in the shoulder, her knuckles cracking hard against solid muscle. Mac staggered back, sputtering.

"Goddammit," he barked, rubbing his arm. "That hurt. Why can't you punch like a girl instead of like a bare-knuckle boxer?"

"Why can't you stop being a meddling, no-good, over-protective bastard of a—"

"Um, guys?" Sam interrupted, stepping between them. Sheri looked at Sam, and Mac followed suit, looking a little more reluctant. "How about we focus on our happy news here instead of your instinct to kill each other?"

"I'm good with that," Sheri said, and hugged her brother again.

"So what is the plan here?" Mac asked, giving Sheri a

squeeze before stepping back to survey them. "Sam? Your military record is clear and untarnished. You're reporting to Kaneohe Bay in a couple weeks, but that's not far from here. Will you drop your letter or—"

"I'm not sure. Not yet anyway, or at least not about my future with the military." He looked down at Sheri, his expression so warm she felt her skin prickle. "That's something I need to discuss with the woman I'd like to make a home with, regardless of where that home ends up being."

"Home," Sheri repeated, thinking she'd never heard a more beautiful word in her whole life.

His blue eyes held hers, and she had to stop herself from throwing herself into his arms all over again.

"I have something for you." Sam reached into his pocket and pulled out an object.

Sheri frowned. "Your night-vision goggles?"

"No, wait." He reached back into the same pocket, this time drawing out an ornate silver brooch in the shape of a devil dog.

Sheri gasped. "What in the world—"

"I found it in a gift shop today. I was going to come back before my flight left to make one more grand gesture. To give it to you as a token of who I really am, in case you're willing make a fresh start together with everything out in the open." He swallowed, emotion flickering in his eyes.

Sheri took the brooch, feeling the warmth of his hand in the metal. She turned it over in her hand and peered at the design. "What does it say on the back—'I'm stuck in you'?"

"Uh, it was supposed to say *on* you—not in you. Like a pin? It was a lame joke. The engraver misunderstood. I can have it redone—"

"No." She clutched it to her chest. "It's perfect just the way it is."

Mac folded his arms over his chest and peered at Sam. "You might need to work on your romantic approach."

"Shut up, Mac," she said as she looked at the brooch again. "It's beautiful, Sam. I can't believe you did this."

"I want us to start over," he said. "You, me, and the boys. A family."

"Absolutely," she whispered. "I love the sound of that."

Mac cleared his throat. "I think this is the part where you apologize for punching me and say thank you for bringing Sam into your life. You can start with either one."

"Go away, Mac," Sheri said, smiling. "Don't you have someplace to be?"

"Actually, I do. Not to overshadow this happy occasion, but I came back here to solicit your wisdom on procuring a connubial companion."

Sheri blinked. "Say what?"

"A wife," Sam said, putting an arm around Sheri. "Or a fiancée or girlfriend or something. Is this like that time I got that antique NTW-20 anti-materiel sniper rifle with the 20-millimeter barrel and you suddenly had to have the same gun?"

Mac snorted, looking indignant. "Of course not. It's a long story. A business proposition, really, which I'll tell you about if one of you would like to join me in the kitchen to rustle up some sort of dinner?"

"Not it!" Sam and Sheri chorused before dissolving into laughter.

She stepped toward the kitchen, grabbing her brother by one arm and Sam by the other, dragging them both with her. "Fine, Mac. We'll make dinner. And we'll arrange your marriage, too, while we're at it. Why don't you tell us all about it?"

She towed the men into the kitchen, her mind already bubbling with this crazy idea in the back of her brain.

She knew just the wife for MacArthur.

And just the way to make him pay.

Acknowlegments

A million thanks to the best critique partners and beta readers a girl could wish for. Cynthia Reese, Linda Grimes, Linda Brundage, Larie Borden, Bridget McGinn, and Minta Powelson — you rock so hard you make me seasick.

I'm eternally thankful to everyone at Entangled Publishing, especially Heather Howland, Liz Pelletier, Kerri-Leigh Grady, Kari Olson, Jacki Rosellen, Jessica Turner, and Tara Gonzalez. Publishing is a team effort, and I'm glad you're in the dugout with me offering wisdom, enthusiasm, and encouraging butt pats.

I'm so grateful to Michelle Wolfson for being the ultimate champion of my career, and for handling all the details that would otherwise make my brain explode. I thank you from the bottom of my heart (not to mention my non-exploded brain).

Huge hugs and thank yous to my family, especially my parents, Dixie and David Fenske. I'm not sure whether to be more grateful for your love and support, or for your decision to live half the year in Kauai so I have the excuse to visit frequently in the name of book research.

And thank you to Craig Zagurski for supporting my writing from, "don't talk, I'm plotting!" to "come quick, I need to see if a guy can unhook a girl's bra when she's kneeling in front of him!" I love you always, babe.

About the Author

Tawna Fenske traveled a career path that took her from newspaper reporter to English teacher in Venezuela to marketing geek to PR manager for her city's tourism bureau. An avid globetrotter and social media fiend, Tawna is the author of the popular blog, Don't Pet Me, I'm Writing, and a member of Romance Writers of America. She lives with her fiancé in Bend, Oregon, where she'll invent any excuse to hike, bike, snowshoe, float the river, or sip wine on her back deck. She's published several romantic comedies with Sourcebooks, Coliloquy, and Entangled Publishing. Her quirky brand of comedy and romance has won praises from *RT Book Reviews*, *Library Journal*, and the *Chicago Tribune*, which noted, "Fenske's wildly inventive plot & wonderfully quirky characters provide the perfect literary antidote to any romance reader's summer reading doldrums."

www.tawnafenske.com

Made in the USA
San Bernardino, CA
30 August 2015